Welcome to the Secret World of Alex Mack!

These days it's hard for all us Macks to get together for a real vacation. But it was finally happening. We were going camping in this gigantic RV, way out in the desert. I was pretty excited about it, but my sister, Annie, wasn't—until Ray suggested she could *really* test my superpowers, and no one would ever know. How much trouble could we get in, all alone, in the middle of nowhere? As it turned out, *a lot*. Let me explain. . . .

I'm Alex Mack. I was just another average kid until my first day of junior high.

One minute I'm walking home from school—the next there's a *crash!* A truck from the Paradise Valley Chemical plant overturns in front of me, and I'm drenched in some weird chemical.

And since then—well, nothing's been the same. I can move objects with my mind, shoot electrical charges through my fingertips, and morph into a liquid shape . . . which is handy when I get in a tight spot!

My best friend, Ray, thinks it's cool—and my sister, Annie, thinks I'm a science project.

They're the only two people who know about my new powers. I can't let anyone else find out—not even my parents—because I know the chemical plant wants to find me and turn me into some experiment.

But you know something? I guess I'm not so ~~av~~ age anymore!

D0402447

The Secret World of Alex Mack™

Alex, You're Glowing!
Bet You Can't!
Bad News Babysitting!
Witch Hunt!
Mistaken Identity!
Cleanup Catastrophe!
Take a Hike!
Go for the Gold!
Poison in Paradise!
Zappy Holidays! (Super Edition)
Junkyard Jitters!
Frozen Stiff!
I Spy!
High Flyer!
Milady Alex!
Father-Daughter Disaster!
Bonjour, Alex!
Close Encounters!

Available from MINSTREL Books

For orders other than by individual consumers, Pocket Books grants a discount on the purchase of **10 or more** copies of single titles for special markets or premium use. For further details, please write to the Vice-President of Special Markets, Pocket Books, 1633 Broadway, New York, NY 10019-6785, 8th Floor.

For information on how individual consumers can place orders, please write to Mail Order Department, Simon & Schuster Inc., 200 Old Tappan Road, Old Tappan, NJ 07675.

NICKELODEON®

the secret world of

ALEX MACK™

Close Encounters!

David Cody Weiss and Bobbi JG Weiss

A MINSTREL® BOOK

Published by POCKET BOOKS

New York   London   Toronto   Sydney   Tokyo   Singapore

The sale of this book without its cover is unauthorized. If you purchased this book without a cover, you should be aware that it was reported to the publisher as "unsold and destroyed." Neither the author nor the publisher has received payment for the sale of this "stripped book."

This book is a work of fiction. Names, characters, places and incidents are products of the author's imagination or are used fictitiously. Any resemblance to actual events or locales or persons, living or dead, is entirely coincidental.

A MINSTREL PAPERBACK *Original*

A Minstrel Book published by
POCKET BOOKS, a division of Simon & Schuster Inc.
1230 Avenue of the Americas, New York, NY 10020

Copyright © 1997 by Viacom International Inc., and RHI Entertainment, Inc. All rights reserved. Based on the Nickelodeon series entitled "The Secret World of Alex Mack."

All rights reserved, including the right to reproduce this book or portions thereof in any form whatsoever. For information address Pocket Books, 1230 Avenue of the Americas, New York, NY 10020

ISBN: 0-671-00706-8

First Minstrel Books printing August 1997

10 9 8 7 6 5 4 3 2 1

NICKELODEON and all related titles, logos and characters are trademarks of Viacom International, Inc.

A MINSTREL BOOK and colophon are registered trademarks of Simon & Schuster Inc.

Cover photos by Thomas Queally and Danny Feld

Printed in the U.S.A.

For George:
"Stick with me, babe, we'll go Place."

Welcome to Place!

CHAPTER 1

"And just how long have you had these . . . *powers?*" the man in the polyester suit sneered.

The young girl squirmed in her chair under the hot lights and didn't answer. Her mother, sitting in the next chair, answered for her. "She doesn't like to talk about it in public. The only reason we're here is that we felt that people should know what happened to us during the . . . *incident* . . . and know how difficult life has been for us since—"

"Since you were all taken away on the alien spaceship," finished the man with a smirk.

"Yo, Alex! Can you believe this stuff?"

"What I can't believe, Ray," said Alex Mack, glaring at her best friend, "is how you're goofing off watching that stupid TV show when you're supposed to be helping to pack all this *stuff* you think you need for this trip!"

Raymond Alvarado tore his eyes away from the television set and glanced at the pile in the middle of the Macks' living room floor. Tumbled around a green duffel bag were sneakers, hiking boots, assorted clothes, fishing gear and an uninflated black rubber inner tube. "Hey, we're going to be out camping for a whole week," he said. "I figure I should be prepared for anything we might think of doing. Hiking, rock climbing, swimming, fishing—"

"Swimming? Fishing?" Alex interrupted. "Ray, we're camping out in the *desert!* Where do you think you're going to find enough water to *fish* in, let alone swim?"

Ray reluctantly knelt on the floor and began stuffing things into his duffel. "You never know what you'll find to do out there," he said. "Maybe we'll meet some kids with a dune buggy who'll take us out racing or something."

"Yeah, right," said Alex skeptically. "And what color is the sky in *your* world today?"

"Laugh now, Al, but *this* cool camper is gonna be prepared for anything." Ray looked back at the TV. "Check this total wack-out. It's where we find out what weird stuff they're going to talk about tomorrow."

The host was leading the audience in laughing and catcalling the guest family as they left the set. Then he turned and looked straight at the camera, adopting an expression of earnest sincerity. "That concludes today's show on alien abductions," he oozed. "Be sure to join us for tomorrow's show—Do Aliens Walk Among Us?" The camera zoomed in for a close-up. "Are there strange beings with mysterious powers living in our cities, our towns, our neighborhoods? Is the person next to you really *human?* Find out tomorrow on 'Exposé with Richard Blather'!"

Alex snapped out of her trance and frowned at the television, annoyed that she'd become just as distracted as Ray. She pointed a finger and fired a sparkling golden zapper at the TV, turning it off. "My folks will be back with the motor

3

home any minute, Ray. We're late enough as it is!"

Ray turned to look at Alex with his eyes open wide and staring. He struck a theatrical pose that Alex presumed was supposed to be shock and horror. "That's it!" he gasped at her. "You didn't get your powers from being soaked in that GC-161 gunk. You're really an alien, sent down here to spy on us poor, defenseless Earthlings!" Alex started to giggle in spite of herself. "You don't morph into liquid goo from your human state—you're actually goo pretending to be a teenage girl!"

The game was so delicious and contagious that Alex got excited and began to glow. She threw herself into the role. From the pile of camping gear she levitated an aluminum pie plate into position over her head like a floating crown. Using her deepest voice she boomed at Ray, "Beware, Earthling! You have discovered the secret no one must know! Now you must pay the price!"

With a wave of her hand, Alex made the top pop off a can of tennis balls and floated three balls in the air. In rapid succession she made them fly at Ray, bonking him on the head. Ray ran for cover. The balls zipped around the living room to pursue Ray from three angles at once. "No one escapes Alien Alex, Queen of Outer Space!"

Ray ducked quickly but got nailed by two of the tennis balls. The third missed and went sailing across the room. It hit Alex's sister square in the stomach just as she came walking in from the kitchen with a stack of plastic cups in her hands. Annie jumped in surprise and the cups dropped to the floor with a clatter.

"Oops," said Ray.

"Double oops," Alex chimed in, returning to her normal color. The pie plate flew back on top of the picnic basket.

"Alex," began Annie crossly, "how many times have I told you—"

"—not to use your powers where people can see you," finished Alex, Ray and Annie in unison.

"Don't get cute with me about it," Annie snapped. "What if it had been Mom or Dad who had walked in instead of me?" She bent down and began picking up the dropped cups.

"Mom and Dad aren't back with the motor home yet, and you know it," said Alex. "What's got *you* grumpy all of a sudden?"

Annie restacked the cups and tucked them neatly into a bag containing other picnic supplies. "Nothing."

"Yeah, right," said Alex. "And I guess 'nothing' is also responsible for the way you're brimming over with enthusiasm about the trip."

Annie frowned at her sister. "Look, I'm sure this will be a week of Great Family Fun." Her eyes glanced fretfully up toward her room upstairs. "But I'm starting college in a few months, and I need all the time I can get to work on my projects."

Alex grabbed her sister by the shoulders. "Whoa! Earth to Annie! This is a *vacation!* You know—time people spend *not* working? Besides, between Dad's schedule at work and Mom's being back in school, it was hard enough for them to arrange to *have* a family vacation."

"Anyway," Ray piped up, "you've always said that Alex was your most special project. You'll have her all to yourself out in the desert! No neighbors to worry about—no Danielle Atron and her goons breathing down Alex's neck—" Ray suddenly shut up as he realized that Alex was staring daggers at him.

But it was too late. Annie's eyes were already gleaming with excitement. "You know, you're right. I could do a complete baseline scan and then see where the limits of Alex's powers are now!" Annie moved quickly toward the stairs, talking to herself. "Ohmigosh! I have a whole bunch of equipment to pack—in a hurry!" She disappeared upstairs.

Ray spread his hands and looked apologetically at Alex. She hissed back at him, "Thanks a lot, Mister Great Ideas. You've just turned my vacation into a field trip as my sister's pet guinea pig." Alex stared at the duffel bag. It rose into the air and hovered over Ray's head. "Maybe I should pack *you* instead of your stuff."

Ray was saved by the rumble of heavy tires on the driveway outside. "Uh-oh! Parent alert!" he yelled, and dove out from under the floating duffel.

As casual as she was about using her powers around Annie and Ray, Alex was still very careful not to let her parents know that their daughter could levitate things, shoot electric zappers and morph into liquid at will. She quickly lowered the duffel to the floor and for good measure, started packing Ray's sports gear into it so she would look busy.

The front door opened and Alex's parents walked in. "Sure, it's more than we'd originally planned," George Mack was explaining to his wife, "but it'll be worth it for the convenience. And don't forget about the possibility of bad weather sometime in the next week."

Barbara Mack threw her hands up in surrender. Alex gave her mother a puzzled look. "What's going on, Mom?"

"Your father got a little . . . carried away at the RV rental place," her mother said. She waved her hand toward the open door. "See for yourself."

Alex and Ray scrambled out to the front lawn, then stood there, mouths hanging open.

In the driveway sat an enormous motor home. At least twenty feet long, it looked like a brightly painted, squared-off bus. Attached to a towbar behind the motor home was a small four-wheel drive, all-terrain car. There was also a large lumpy object fastened to the back of the motor home and covered with a blue plastic tarp.

Ray was stunned at the sight of the 4WD. "Cool," he said. He shot a superior glance at Alex. "It's as good as a dune buggy." Alex pouted and tried to ignore the jab.

George Mack had entered, but missed the exchange of looks between the kids. "It's the most practical of solutions," he started to explain in a reasonable tone. Fingers ticked off points. "A large, comfortable home base, room enough for shelter in case of inclement weather, *plus* a utility vehicle to provide mobility and fuel cost savings over moving the Runnamucka around on short trips—"

"The *what?*" said Alex, giggling.

"Oh," said her father, looking slightly sheepish. "That's what I used to call them when I was your age."

"This is just too cool," said Ray as he clapped his hands in joyous amazement. "We're going out to the desert with a dune buggy and a Runnamucka!" He beamed at Alex's father. "Way to go, Mr. Mack!"

CHAPTER 2

Alex had anticipated that driving out to the desert would be a great and exciting adventure. And it might have been—if she'd been awake for any of the drive.

Everyone was up and bustling hours before dawn. Everyone, that is, except Alex. She stumbled around like a zombie, rubbing her bleary eyes and chain-yawning. She tried to help with the final preparations but ended up spending less time getting things done than simply trying not to get run over by busier people. Even Ray was ready, arriving from his house next door

cheerful and bouncing with energy and efficiency. He headed straight for the older Macks.
"Dad really appreciates your letting me come
along on your trip," he said. He cast a wistful
glance back at his own home. "I just wish that
he wasn't so busy that we couldn't do something together."

George Mack clapped an arm around the boy's
shoulder. "We're always glad to have you
along, Ray."

Ray smiled his thanks and trotted off to help
with the last-minute loading.

At last the final checking and double-checking
of the house was complete. Every gas switch and
faucet had been turned off and every door and
window was locked. George and Barbara Mack
climbed into the front seats of the Runnamucka
as the three kids settled themselves into the rear.
Carefully, Alex's father backed out of the driveway and set the lumbering motor home on a
course for the highway. Alex rested her head
against a side window and watched her pre-
dawn neighborhood slide away in the darkness.

The next thing she knew, Annie was digging
an elbow in her side. Bright light stung her eyes

as she opened them. Her father called back from the driver's seat, "We'll be passing through Dryrot in just a few minutes, kids. Last outpost of civilization between here and our campsite."

"Dryrot?" Ray laughed. "Who'd ever name a town Dryrot?"

"Lots of old towns in the West have colorful or eccentric names," Barbara Mack said. "It's all part of the charm." Her eyes sparkled as she gazed out at the landscape. "Just by looking around you can almost see history. Think of the strength and the bravery of the pioneers who originally settled here."

All Alex could see was mile after mile of rocky desert peppered with scrubby brown plants shimmering under a blazing sun. She could feel the heat radiating from the window glass. "Maybe we should stop in town and make sure we have enough ice and cold drinks," she suggested.

"Oh, I think we have enough to last us," said George Mack. "Besides, that's the town right ahead." He pointed toward a single sprawling wooden building. It had a corrugated metal roof over weatherbeaten walls. Signs advertising soft drinks, gasoline and auto repair had faded to blurred pastel tones. Several pickup trucks sat in no particular order in front of the covered porch that ran along the front.

"That's a town?" said Alex in disbelief.

"It's got all the basic components of small-town civilization," said her father over his shoulder. "Post office, gas station, general store, cafe and town hall"—he flashed a smile at Alex—"all conveniently located in the same building."

Alex was amazed. Did her dad just make a joke?

"Must be crowded when everybody comes to town at once," cracked Ray.

"Probably not, Ray," said George. "The average population density out here can't be more than, say, two point three people per ten square miles. If you wanted to really get away from the hustle and bustle of suburban living, this is the area to do it."

Alex was relieved. That sounded more like the Dad she knew.

Alex peered out at the desert landscape, then glanced over at Annie. If she was going to have to play guinea pig for her sister, at least this seemed like a safe place to cut loose without worrying about witnesses.

The town disappeared into the distance behind them as the Runnamucka wound its way through a series of low hills. The road grew steeper as they drove along the narrow canyon cut by a long-dry streambed. Hairpin turns became more common and Alex heard her father shift twice into lower gears.

The motor home labored its way up a final grade. Suddenly it didn't look at all like they were a few thousand feet above sea level. A scrubby dry landscape stretched miles ahead, as level as a countertop. In the far distance the purple wedges of a mountain range formed the horizon. "Welcome to the high desert," announced George Mack.

Alex had always thought of deserts as low flat areas where nothing lived. To her they were just barren wastes that simply filled the spaces between more comfortable terrain. The idea of going up into a mountainous area to find a flat desert on top made her head swim a little. She looked out at the mountain range in the distance and had a flash of climbing them and finding another flat desert up there. And the mountains beyond that would have flat deserts on them. It made her think of stacked layers, like a wedding cake.

And she was wrong about there being no life up here. During the drive between the final pass and their camp area she discovered that the desert was not at all deserted.

Sure, the plants that grew up here weren't as dense and pretty as what she saw at home, but everywhere she looked there were big, burly bushes, punctuated by spiky plants with colorful flowers on tall stalks. A brief memory of science class ran through her mind and she found names to attach to those plants. They were yuccas, and the bushy things would be sage plants and chaparral.

The noise of the big motor home rumbling along the narrow blacktop road spooked animals left and right as it passed. Alex had never imagined that so many jackrabbits, prairie dogs and birds lived here. Every so often they passed a sudden cut in the flat of the desert, sometimes with a dry streambed at its bottom, but more rarely with a living stream. The stream-fed ravines were crowded with plants that took advantage of the scarce water and made dense green threads in the tan landscape. At one stream Alex saw a deerlike creature lift its head from drinking to stare placidly at the Runnamucka rolling by. It showed no fear, only mild curiosity at the passing of this alien creature through its territory. The desert had a lot more going for it than Alex realized.

The camping area lay nestled in the bend of a ravine with a small but lively stream running along its bottom. A large level area had been scooped out of the hillside and was furnished with concrete pads, redwood picnic tables and local-stone fire pits. A pair of portapotties stood at the far end of the campground. There were no other campers or motor homes parked there, and George Mack crowed as he parked the Runnamucka, "Great! Looks like we've got the place to ourselves!"

Alex, Ray and Annie scrambled out of the vehicle to check out their home for the next week. Alex walked over to the edge of the ravine and looked down at the stream, a little disappointed that there were no deer to be seen, like at the other stream.

Ray joined her, gazing down at the coolness below. He then turned back to the motor home as Alex's parents stepped out, slowly stretching their stiff legs. "Hey, Mr. M.," Ray said, pointing to the ravine floor. "How come the camp isn't down there, where there's shade and water?"

George Mack ambled over to the edge and looked down. "Too dangerous to camp down there," he said.

"Too *what?*" said Ray with a laugh. "Do fish come out at night and mug campers?"

Alex's father squinted carefully at the stream as if measuring. "Too small for fish, I think," he said. "But that's not the danger. The real problem is flash floods."

"Floods in the desert?" exclaimed Alex. "Most of this area doesn't look like it's seen rain in centuries."

"You're almost right," said her father. "Precipitation in the desert is probably less than an inch a year." He pointed north toward the mountains, barely visible above the rim of the ravine. "But there are frequent thunderstorms up in that range, and the water runs down the hillsides and out into the desert. That's how all these ravines and arroyos got here—cut into the high desert by flooding water, always looking for the easiest route downhill. By the time all those little streams come together into one big one, it can create a wall of water that moves faster than a freight train."

Alex looked at the scoured walls of the ravine and tried to imagine it filled with roiling, muddy water. "Then why are we camped here at all?" she asked, unconsciously stepping back from the edge.

Her father was already heading back to the motor home as he answered. "Nothing to worry about, really, Alex. All you have to do is remember to stay out of ravines if you know it's raining in the mountains. Now give us a hand with unpacking."

Alex and Ray followed him. "Maybe I should just hang out here for the whole trip," Alex said.

"I think you'd have to take that up with your sister, Al," Ray said. "She looks like she's planning something already."

Alex glanced over at Annie. Her sister was

squinting up at the sun, shading her eyes with one hand. In the other hand she held an unfolded map. She turned to Alex and Ray. "It's only about noon," she said. "If you two move faster than snails, we can be unpacked in an hour and still have time to go on a scouting hike."

"You want to start *today?*" moaned Alex in dismay. "But it's hot, and we've got all your electronic junk to haul around."

"Yeah," said Ray. "Hiking can be a lot of fun, but not if I've got to be a pack mule while doing it."

"Look," said Annie, a steely glint in her eye, "you got me to go on this trip because you promised we could do tests. To do tests, I've got to have my equipment. So unless you want to show off in front of *them*"—she jerked a thumb at her parents, who were unhitching the 4WD from the back of the motor home—"we have to carry the stuff ourselves."

Alex's face fell as she pictured herself staggering through the desert under a backpack nearly as tall as she was. Ray tried to cheer her up. "It won't be so bad," he said. "As soon as we're out of sight, you can float everything and not have to strain a muscle.''

"No way,'' interrupted Annie. "I want fresh and accurate measurements. Levitation along the way will use up too much of her strength.''

Alex was about to reject the whole idea, which she knew would start a fight with Annie and probably ruin the entire vacation, when her father called from the back of the Runnamucka. "Hey, kids, here's the surprise I promised you. Come on back here.''

Alex was grateful to be saved from having to answer Annie. She hustled quickly to join her parents, who were untying the rope holding the mysterious blue plastic tarp to the back of the motor home. Ray ran to the far side and grabbed a corner of the tarp, ready to pull when they told him to.

"On a count of three,'' said Mr. Mack. "One . . . two . . . three!'' The blue tarp floated in midair for a moment, then fell to the ground, exposing three small, brightly painted bicycles with heavy, knobbly tires.

"Trail bikes!'' crowed Ray. "Too cool!''

George Mack beamed at the amazed stares from the three teenagers. "I thought you'd like them," he said. "This should make getting around a breeze for you."

Alex caught Annie's look of triumph. She was doomed to play guinea pig after all.

CHAPTER 3

It took Alex, Annie and Ray much longer to set up camp and pack for a hike than Annie had predicted. Before they could even start, the kids had to help the adults convert the Runnamucka from a motor home to a camp base. An hour later, Barbara Mack was still moving aluminum chairs around under the extended awning, searching for the "perfect" arrangement. George Mack took pity on the impatient youngsters and gave them permission to head out. Without looking up from her task, his wife called out, "I'm planning to have dinner at sunset, so make sure you're back in time to help!"

"No problem, Mom!" yelled Alex as she vanished around the corner of the motor home.

With the adults preoccupied, the kids felt safe in assembling the gear for their outing on the far side of the Runnamucka. Annie, efficient as usual, had put most of her equipment into her backpack before leaving the house. Alex and Ray had to dump out their backpacks in order to repack and make room for Annie's surplus widgets.

Alex had thought that having trail bikes would make lugging heavy packs around the desert less of a burden. She hadn't counted on her sister's love of efficiency. "Since we have the bikes now," Annie announced, "we can carry all my gear together and set it up in one trip."

Ray took this news the hardest. "How am I going to carry all of your stuff and mine in one pack?"

Annie cocked an eyebrow at him. "What's the problem? Just take along the stuff you think is vital for this trip and leave the rest."

"But it's *all* vital," moaned Ray. "Since I don't know what I might find to do out there, I have to bring everything, just to be prepared."

Alex knew her best friend too well, so she let

Annie pop the obvious question. "What do you mean by 'everything'?"

Ray started pulling items out of his duffel and spreading them out on the ground. "Well," he began, "I've got the sports gear, of course—baseball, bat and mitt, frisbee, kite supplies, my exploration stuff—compass, campstove, binoculars, pitons, rope, safari hat, gold panning setup and metal detector—"

"Gold panning?" interrupted Annie. "*Metal detector?* What kind of trip are you planning for, Ray?"

"That's just it," said Ray seriously. "There's so many things to do out here, I don't want to miss out on anything. I pride myself on being prepared."

Annie rolled her eyes in exasperation. "You can conquer the wilderness later in the week, Ray. Right now you're part of the deal that Alex made. First you help with testing—*then* you play Lewis and Clark."

Ray looked for help from Alex, but she just shrugged in a "that's Annie" gesture. So the two of them set to work stocking their backpacks with Annie's widgetry and their own gear.

Alex poked Ray in the ribs. "A metal detector?"

She snickered. "Where'd you get a metal detector and what did you expect to find with it?"

"It's not a big one," said Ray, pulling a metal disk attached to a collapsible handle out of his duffel. "Just a portable one that my uncle uses to trace out lost water and gas pipes. He loaned it to me for the trip. Anyway, this used to be old mining country. I could find an overlooked vein of silver or gold and strike it rich!"

"Right," said Alex. "If you get rich on *my* family's camping trip, then dinner's on you—forever." She topped off her pack with a compass and a copy of the survey map for the area that Annie had downloaded from the Internet. Even with the extra weight of Annie's widgets, the pack's sturdy aluminum frame hung easily from Alex's shoulders and just cleared the back of the trail bike when she sat on its seat.

Finally preparations were done. Annie studied her map and took a direction fix with her compass. She looked up and pointed westward. "There's a spot about five miles that way that looks like it might be what we need."

"Need to do what?" asked George Mack as he rounded the corner of the Runnamucka.

Annie was caught off-guard, for once. Alex cut in with, "Where we need to be in order to see the biggest variety of . . . rock formations."

George Mack looked puzzled. "If it was rock formations you wanted to see, you should have told us. We could have gone to Bryce Canyon or the Painted Desert."

Alex smiled broadly at her dad. "That would have been great for Annie, 'cause she's a genius and all," she said. "But Ray and I are only beginners and need to stay with simple stuff."

Her father considered this for a moment and then nodded. "Very wise, Alex. However, don't underestimate this area. There are some pretty unusual minerals and ores to be found around here." Ray shot a triumphant look at Alex as her father continued, "The locals swear there's something in these hills that turns compasses funny and makes people get lost. Keep careful track of the sun and landmarks."

They all assured him that they would and then tore out of the campground in a flash, raising rooster tails of dust in their wake.

As they raced through the desert, dodging rocky outcrops and brush, Alex called out to her sister, "What's so special about this Fantasmas Mesa place that's worth the five miles we're pedaling?"

Annie swerved her bike to a stop and waved at the land in front of them. "It's a perfect site. It's a shallow box canyon cutting into a mesa, which means we're shielded on three sides by cliffs. There are plenty of loose boulders around to lift for strength tests. *And* there's a streambed in a ravine around the bend over there where we can wash up before we head back." She started unloading her backpack. "In short, a place where you can cut loose without fear and we can continue to research what that GC-161 is doing to your body."

In spite of herself, Alex shivered a little at the mention of GC-161. On her first day of junior high school, a delivery truck for Paradise Valley Chemical had nearly run her down. She had dodged out of its way, but the truck had crashed into a fire hydrant, dumping barrels of its chemical cargo. Alex had been soaked in a shower of golden goo—GC-161—before she'd fled the scene.

Alex soon discovered that the GC-161 had

transformed her life forever. Her body would give off a golden glow when she was embarrassed and it could generate electric "zappers" of varying power which she could shoot from her fingers. The strangest effect was that by concentrating, she could morph into a clear liquid—a liquid she could make move through pipes or the thinnest of spaces. Next to that, her ability to levitate objects and project force fields felt almost "normal" by now.

Annie, being a scientific genius, had identified GC-161 as the cause of Alex's transformation and had assigned herself the task of analyzing Alex's powers. As much as Alex felt like a guinea pig, she was still grateful to have someone who knew what had happened to her and who could figure out solutions when things went wrong—which happened far too often for Alex's taste.

Ray also knew about Alex's powers, but he could care less about the whys of them. To him Alex was still his best friend and it was up to him and Annie to help keep her powers a secret from everybody else. Especially from Danielle Atron and her company, Paradise Valley Chemical.

PVC had made GC-161 illegally and in strictest secrecy. Their highest priority was to discover the identity of the child who was at the truck accident and snatch him or her for extensive experiments. The thought of life in a bell jar in Danielle Atron's labs gave Alex good reason to shiver when she thought of GC-161. Her only hope of continued safety lay in her ability to control and conceal her powers until she could figure out how to handle the consequences of being "the GC-161 kid." Alex was big on the "control" part of that job, while Annie continually stressed the "conceal" part.

The three teenagers emptied out their backpacks and set to work positioning Annie's sensors and testing devices. Ray positioned each device while Alex sat and sorted out what seemed like miles of wire and cabling—all coiled, tied and neatly labeled in Annie's precise writing—and laid them out so Annie could connect the sensors to her laptop computer.

Finally everything was ready. Using an empty backpack for a cushion, Ray leaned back against a rock and folded his arms behind his head. "All right," he beamed. "Let's see some fireworks." Alex's fingers tingled in anticipation.

Annie shot him a dark look. "Get real, Ray," she said. "These are scientific tests. We're going to start with all the baseline readings and then proceed to do incremental progressions until we reach Alex's limits." Annie lifted up a small Mason jar with some capsules in it. "Then," she continued, "since we know that cayenne pepper increases some of Alex's powers, I want to do the whole series over again after she eats some pepper."

"You're not going to make me eat some of Mom's curry sauce again, are you?" Alex groaned. Barbara Mack was a creative, if unconventional, cook and was always surprising her family with some exotic recipe for dinner. Once she'd made an extra-hot batch of curry sauce and Alex discovered that it unexpectedly gave her superstrength—but only for a while.

"No curry sauce," promised Annie. "Mom knows we hated it so she swore not to make it again." She held up the Mason jar. "I brought along pure cayenne pepper!"

Alex jumped up in alarm. "No way!" she

shouted. "I'm not burning my tongue off! Not for science—not for anything!"

Annie looked exasperated. "You don't have to burn anything, Alex," she said calmly, rattling the jar. "I put the pepper in some gel capsules. You won't taste it at all."

At this news, Alex calmed down, but it was now Ray's turn to get upset. "Does 'incremental progressions' mean what I think it does?" He rolled his eyes. "I'm supposed to sit here and watch you guys lift pebbles in size order—and then do it all over again?" He screwed his face up into a lemon-sucking expression. "*Not* my idea of fun in the desert."

Alex wasn't too thrilled at the idea either, but a deal was a deal.

"You can go explore or prospect or whatever it is you want to do until we're done for today," Annie told Ray. "Just don't get lost."

Ray stood up and struck what he imagined was a "rugged pioneer" pose. "Hey, I read up on desert survival. You're looking at a first-class explorer. This'll be a snap."

Alex looked at Ray wistfully. "Have fun," she said. "Find me a gold nugget or two, okay?"

31

Ray grinned and shrugged into his backpack. He waved good-bye and headed west into the maze of chaparral.

Annie handed Alex a set of small white discs with gleaming metal centers. "Put these electrodes on. They'll monitor your vital signs. Then we can get started."

Alex sighed. It was going to be a long afternoon.

But after they got started, it wasn't as bad as she'd feared. Faster than Alex expected, she and Annie covered most of the strength tests. Things got really interesting when Alex found out that Annie wanted to focus on dexterity testing next.

Annie's main goal was to see how many things Alex could do at once. Alex's mood lightened and she suddenly felt a freedom she'd never felt before. *It must be the desert*, she thought. *I don't have to be cautious and hide my powers. I can just cut loose and have fun!* She threw herself into the tests, taking each one as a challenge and trying to push herself to her limits.

They started simply—how many objects could Alex levitate at the same time? One by one she floated pebbles into the air until there were literally dozens of them weaving an intricate dance a hundred feet overhead. The girls found out that it wasn't the number of objects that tired her out, but the total mass of whatever she was lifting. Pebbles were a snap, but she could lift far fewer fist-size rocks, and only a couple of real boulders without tiring.

"Now look away," Annie instructed, as Alex juggled several rocks of different sizes. Alex averted her eyes and heard a chorus of thumps as the rocks plummeted back to earth. "Just what I thought," said Annie, typing furiously into her laptop. "You have to keep what you're doing directly in sight to control it. No lifting things around corners—yet."

Alex took a breather for a few minutes and then worked on mixing levitation with zappers. She floated rocks high into the air and fired zappers at them, knocking the weightless rocks into each other. "This is like playing midair billiards," she said, giggling.

"Mmm-hmmn," muttered Annie, completely absorbed in entering data.

Alex decided to use her sister's distraction to really have some fun. *I wonder if I can skywrite my name?* she thought. Frowning with concentration, she lifted dozens of small rocks at once and began forming them into her name. In letters fifty feet tall the word *Alex* started to take shape.

By themselves, the rocks were barely visible. Alex thought that they needed a little sparkle, so she sent up a stream of zappers to hit the rocks and burst into tiny twinkles. *It's like aiming a hose that sprays light,* she thought. Though the zappers' glow faded rapidly, Alex could still make a golden trail in the sky that ran over the rocks spelling out her name.

Alex was just painting the *x* with zappers when a hoarse shouting broke the silence of the desert. Her concentration shattered and the rocks plummeted to the ground as the shouting came closer.

Alex and Annie looked at each other in shock as they recognized the voice that was so filled with fear and panic—it was Ray's!

CHAPTER 4

Alex and Annie ran toward the sound of Ray's voice, dodging around boulders and ducking under sprawling sage bushes. They couldn't make out what he was shouting about, but it was obvious that he was in some kind of trouble. As Ray's voice grew louder, Alex could hear a strange humming sound growing louder as well.

Suddenly Ray came into view, running at top speed toward them. Instead of stopping, however, he ran right past Alex and Annie, back the way they had come. The strange humming was louder now and Ray was already past the girls by the time Alex realized that Ray was shouting, "Helllp! Waaassspsss!"

And wasps there were. Not twenty feet behind Ray boiled a dark cloud of angry insects, weaving their way around bushes and rocks like a single vengeful organism, bent on venting their fury on the boy—or anyone else in their way.

Without thinking, Alex threw up a force shield and moved it to block the wasps' path. The insects slammed into the invisible disk and roiled about in confusion, but only for a moment. Alex could see individual wasps zip in and out of the main cloud and come close to the shield's edge. Eventually one would find the edge and fly past. The rest would quickly follow.

Alex extended the shield as wide as she could and watched the rim anxiously. Each time the boiling mass of wasps threatened to spill out of the shield she fired a zapper at that edge to drive the insects back. She yelled to her sister, "Annie! Quick! How do you calm down wasps?"

"Smoke!" Annie shouted back. "Beekeepers use smoke to sedate bees when they collect honey!"

"We don't have any smoke," cried Alex as she

watched the mass of wasps flatten against her shield, pushing by sheer numbers toward the edges in spite of the exploding zappers. "What else?"

Annie racked her brain at top speed. "Cold!" she shouted. "Cold puts them to sleep! Push them high up into the atmosphere where it's cold and they'll slow down!"

And maybe they'll wind up too far away to find us again, thought Alex. She reached out with her mind and bent her force shield into a cup shape and pushed as hard as she could. In seconds, the flattened swarm of wasps was hundreds of feet in the air and heading south. But the strain of dealing with the wasps after a long afternoon of stretching her powers to their limits took its toll on Alex. The world suddenly spun around her.

Hands grabbed her, gently steadying her. "It's okay, Alex," Annie's voice said in her ear. "The wasps are gone. You can relax now."

Ray came running up to the girls. He had turned back as soon as he'd realized that Alex and Annie weren't behind him. Alex felt like she'd battled the wasps for hours, but the whole attack had lasted only seconds.

"Way to go, Alex!" crowed Ray. "I knew you could handle those pesky little stingers."

"Which is why you left us here alone to deal with them?" Annie snorted.

Ray grinned in embarrassment. "I didn't exactly *leave* . . ." he said, waving his hands. "It was more like I was moving so fast it took me a while to throw it into reverse, you know?"

Annie cocked an eyebrow at Ray. "And just *why* were those wasps chasing you?"

Ray looked sheepish. "I guess they got mad when my boomerang hit their nest."

"Your *what?*" said Annie, her jaw dropping. Alex tried not to laugh but only succeeded in making a snorting sound.

Ray rolled his eyes and spread his hands. "Well . . . you guys were taking your time with those tests and I got bored searching the ground for gold nuggets, so I decided to try out my boomerang. There's no good place back home where it's safe to throw it. Anyway, I threw it and sorta missed it on its way back. Next thing I know, I hear what sounds like a train heading at me. I just started running as fast as I could." He looked straight at Alex. "Thanks, Al."

Alex took her friend by the arm. "It was a close one for all of us, Ray," she said. "Let's call it a day and pack up."

Annie glanced down at her wrist compass and took a bearing on the sun. She struck off to retrace their path as Alex and Ray trailed behind.

"You know," said Ray, "I wish someone could have timed my run back there. I probably broke an Olympic record or two."

Alex snorted again.

The mountains to the west were gnawing into the bottom of the sun by the time Alex, Annie and Ray made it back to camp. The Runnamucka was dark, but a propane lantern shone on the redwood table. A note was taped to the lantern's handle, and it fluttered in the cooling breeze.

Annie pulled it free, reading it in the lantern's light. "Mom and Dad went to Dryrot to get ice," she told the others. "They want us to start a fire in the pit and set the table."

"Ice?" said Ray. "But didn't your dad say that you already had ice?"

The two Mack girls looked at Ray, quiet smiles quirking up the corners of their mouths. Then

Ray remembered just how absentminded George Mack could be. He laughed out loud. "I guess no trip is complete unless you forget *something.*"

Annie took charge of pouring out charcoal and lighting the fire while Alex and Ray washed up. Then Alex set the table while Ray scraped and cleaned the grill before setting it back on the stones of the fire pit.

Soon headlight beams sliced through the twilight as the Macks' 4WD pulled up behind the Runnamucka. Alex's parents clambered out, each carrying two large sacks of ice.

Everyone was starving, so conversation became secondary to preparing and wolfing down the first family desert cookout. It wasn't until after dinner, with the adults sunk into lounge chairs and the kids crouched in front of the fire roasting marshmallows on sticks that Barbara Mack asked, "And how did your little expedition go today?"

"Great, Mom," answered Alex. "We rode around a lot and Annie got to show off how much she knows."

Annie shot a dark look at her sister for this crack, and Alex just smiled sweetly back.

Her father, as usual, missed this byplay and chimed in cheerily. "Nature is wonderful up close, isn't it? That reminds me, kids, have you picked out where you're going to sleep tonight?"

"In the Runnamucka, of course," said Alex. "Where else?"

"Oh, no, sweetheart," her father said, surprised. "Your mom and I are sleeping there. You kids get to sleep out under the stars in your sleeping bags."

Alex saw Ray and her sister grinning at her. Obviously, they had known about this long before and had been just waiting for Alex to discover it. Alex hated being caught by surprise. She turned back to her father. "There is such a thing as getting *too* close to Nature, Dad," she objected. "If we sleep outside, all sorts of bugs and crawly things can get to us."

Annie started ticking off fingers. "And that's not counting the snakes, and the scorpions, and the 'possums, and the coyotes . . ."

Barbara Mack interrupted. "Stop trying to scare your sister, Annie. You know very well that there isn't going to be any problem like that

41

out here at all. You're going to have a perfectly safe night."

"Unless the 'aliens' get you, that is," her husband said, grinning.

"Aliens?" said all three kids in unison.

"Certainly," said George Mack, ignoring his wife's glare. "While we were in town, we had it on good authority that there's an alien landing base near here."

"What your father *really* means," Barbara Mack said tartly, "is that an old fellow who spent too much time in the sun was telling everybody in town he'd seen a UFO by Fantasmas Mesa this afternoon."

Alex, Annie and Ray exchanged nervous glances. "Did anyone believe him?"

"Of course not," snorted Barbara Mack. "Your father is just pulling your leg. What kind of person would take a story like that seriously?"

"Well," began George Mack, "I knew somebody once—"

"Never mind, George," snapped his wife. "I'm not going to let you fill their heads with ghost stories just before going to bed." She stood up and tugged at his sleeve. "And to make sure of it, you and I should get ready for bed ourselves. We want to get an early start tomorrow."

The elder Macks disappeared into the motor home, closing the door behind them. Without speaking, Annie opened up a storage compartment in the side of the vehicle and pulled out three sleeping bags. Everyone kept silent until the bags were set up around the fire and the light went out in the Runnamucka.

"Do you think that old guy actually saw us?" Alex finally whispered.

"I don't *think* so," Annie whispered back, though without much conviction.

"He said he saw a UFO, not a kid making things float," said Ray encouragingly.

Alex brightened. "You're probably right, Ray. If he'd actually seen us, he'd have been telling people about aliens chasing a screaming teenager through the desert."

"I wasn't really scared," said Ray, trying to be offhanded about his adventure. "I was just reacting in a manner appropriate to the threat."

Alex snickered at him.

"And that's what *we* have to do," Annie suddenly announced. The others looked at her quizzically. "I mean, we can't continue if there are potential observers hiding out in the desert. I'll have to forgo the rest of our tests."

Alex knew better than to comment, but Ray jumped in with both feet. "You mean we get to play around for the rest of the week? Great!"

"I'm glad you think so," said Annie, before sinking into a glum silence.

Alex felt sorry for her sister but didn't really mind not playing guinea pig for the rest of the week. She fluffed her pillow, snuggled down into her sleeping bag and was out like a light in minutes. But her sleep was haunted by visions of being in some sort of cage and having giant fingers poking at her.

CHAPTER 5

The first disadvantage Alex discovered about "outdoor life" was that it started too early. As soon as the sun crested the eastern hills she fought a doomed struggle to stay asleep. She squirmed deeper into her sleeping bag, but the light followed her down and the rising heat threatened to turn the bag into an Alex-size steamer. She finally surrendered and sat up, bleary-eyed and yawning.

"We were wondering if you were going to wake up at all today, sleepyhead," said her mother, who was setting a frying pan down on the fire pit grill. The smell of sizzling bacon brought Alex a little closer to consciousness.

"Yeah, Al," said Ray, stirring a pitcher of orange juice. "The sun's been up for at least an hour. I wanted to get an early start. Today's the day I'm gonna find a gold mine."

Alex surrendered to the inevitable and crawled out of her sleeping bag. As she staggered to her feet, her sister bounded out of the Runnamucka with her wet hair wrapped in a towel turban. "I left you some hot water." Annie smiled. Then added, "Though I think a cold shower might be more effective."

Alex stumbled on toward the shower. *How can all these people be so* cheery *this early in the morning?* she thought.

Twenty minutes and two glasses of orange juice later, Alex had struck a truce with the morning and was starting to plan out her day— her first real, no-worries-no-cares *vacation* day. She had barely scheduled a late-morning nap when Ray shouted, "Hey! Somebody's coming!"

Alex shaded her eyes and looked in the direction Ray was pointing. A rising trail of dust traced the approach of a vehicle. A minute later, a dark, anonymous van pulled up behind the 4WD.

Ray's shout brought the other three Macks out of the motor home. They reached Alex and Ray just as the van's doors opened and two people in dark suits and sunglasses stepped out. The shorter figure was a woman who was talking into a cellular phone. The taller figure was a gangling man. He called out, "Are you the Mack family?" A shield appeared in the man's hand. "We're Special Agents. FBI."

George Mack instinctively stepped in front of his family, his arms spread slightly. "We're the Macks," he said. "Is there some kind of problem? I've got our camping permits if you need to see them."

"I'm sure that any papers filled out by George Mack would be in perfect order," said the man as he walked closer and removed his sunglasses. "I don't remember him ever turning in sloppy work."

George Mack peered ahead, brow furrowed in thought. "Lupo . . . ?" he finally said.

"Right answer, straight out of the gate," said Special Agent Lupo.

George reached out to pump the agent's hand. "You old bloodhound! I haven't seen you in years! What are you doing out in the middle of the desert?" His smile slipped into a look of concern. "You didn't show up here just to greet a long-lost friend. Is this official business?"

Agent Lupo didn't answer. Instead, he made a "hang-on-a-minute" gesture and turned to his partner. She finished talking on her cell phone and snapped it closed. When she joined them, Lupo began introductions. "Special Agent Cabeza, I'd like you to meet George Mack, a whiz at scientific analysis but a complete washout at picking out a matching pair of socks."

"I still can't," said George, shaking Cabeza's hand. He let go and tugged his wife forward. "But I have help now. This is my wife, Barbara, and my daughters, Annie and Alex."

"And I'm Raymond Alvarado, Special Agents," said Ray, reaching out and shaking each agent's hand firmly. "FBI, eh? You know, I've often given thought to pursuing a career in the Bureau. I can see myself as a deep-cover agent, trained in secret combat—"

"I'm afraid it's a lot more humdrum than

that," interrupted Agent Cabeza. "Most of our work is totally mundane—interviews, filling out paperwork, filing. Dull stuff."

"Which brings me to the reason we came out here this morning," said Agent Lupo, looking at the Macks. "We're here to investigate a UFO sighting."

"You're joking, of course," Barbara Mack said.

"Not at all, ma'am," said Agent Cabeza, deadpan. "We work out of an office charged with the investigation of unexplained phenomena. We're not supposed to form opinions, just collect the data."

"Of course," followed up Agent Lupo, a strange light growing in his eyes, "a large proportion of our findings do suggest exotic origins for many of our cases. We've never been able to put all the pieces together at the same time, but I'm sure that someday we'll find the truth we're looking for."

"We heard about yesterday's sighting and drove right out," said Cabeza. "We were already nearby, checking out Area Fifty-one in Nevada."

Ray did a double take. "You mean that place

where they do secret projects that nobody's supposed to know about?"

"Some people believe that," agreed Lupo.

"Heck, that's nothing," said Ray with a sudden grin. "We've got one of them back home. It's called the Paradise Valley Chemical Plant."

Annie elbowed Ray in the ribs. "No making jokes about *my dad's employer*, Ray!"

"Don't be so serious, dear," said Barbara Mack pleasantly. She turned to Agent Lupo. "You say you've worked with George before?"

"Yes ma'am," said Lupo.

"Before we met, honey," George Mack told his wife. "We were undergrads together and we worked on—"

Lupo waggled a cautionary finger. "Uh-uhn."

George Mack blinked. "Oh, right. Secret." He looked back at his wife. "Well, I can tell you about the time I solved his problem with . . . Oops, no I can't. Maybe the job with . . . Drat! Not that either." He spread his hands helplessly. "But he is an old friend. Really."

"The best friend I never had," Lupo assured Barbara Mack, the hint of a smile playing around his lips. "When I accessed the camping reservations database to find the campground nearest to the sighting, I recognized your name on the list. Not stopping by seemed out of the question.''

Alex studied the two agents as they chatted with her parents. Agent Cabeza was a petite woman, no taller than Alex herself. But she seemed to be made of spring steel and precision components, an efficiently humming machine with practically styled, raven black hair.

Agent Lupo presented a contradiction of images. He had a boyish face on a tall, gangling body, but his manner was anything but childish. He had a focused energy in him that lit his eyes. Alex got the impression of someone trying to look in two directions at once as if when he saw things, he tried to see *through* them, looking beyond for something that couldn't be perceived by vision alone.

Alex snapped out of her reverie when she heard Annie say, ''Gee, it was nice meeting you and all, but I'm supposed to lead Alex and Ray on a sort of bike-hike. Maybe if you ever get to Paradise Valley, we'll see you again.''

''Oh, sooner than that, Annie,'' said her father.

He turned to the agents. "Lupo, why don't you share our camp while you look around the desert?"

"Thank you, George. We'll take you up on that. It'll save us a hundred-mile commute from the nearest motel." Agent Lupo smiled at Annie. "We won't be a bother, I promise. We're going out to survey the desert today. You won't even know we're around."

"Sure. Right," said Annie, suddenly uncomfortable. "Well, good luck. We've got to go now." She grabbed Alex and Ray by their sleeves and tugged them to the far side of the camp.

"A sort of *bike-hike?*" asked Ray in confusion. "What were you talking about?"

"I'm sorry," snapped Annie. "I couldn't think of anything any faster. We've got to get on our bikes and get out of here *right now!*"

"I'm not going anywhere until you tell me what's going on," said Alex.

Exasperated, Annie hissed, "Those special agents are here because someone saw *us* doing our tests yesterday! All my equipment is still set up back at Fantasmas Mesa. We've got to go get it before they find it!" She grasped Alex by her shoulders and spoke earnestly. "If we were afraid of what might happen if Danielle Atron found out about you, there's no telling how much worse it could be if the *government* found out. We've got to make sure they don't find *anything!*"

Alex and Ray finally understood what was at stake. They raced their bikes at top speed up to Fantasmas Mesa and packed all of Annie's gear away. At a more leisurely pace, they wound a meandering path back to the camp, circling it once to make sure that the agents' car was gone. Fortunately, the elder Macks were gone as well, so Annie had no trouble repacking her equipment into the farthest corner of the Runnamucka's luggage compartment.

The rest of the day passed into evening without their seeing the agents again. George and Barbara Mack came back from a desert drive in time for another sunset dinner. Alex was soon happy to fall into the comfort of her sleeping bag, bugs or no bugs.

CHAPTER 6

Even before the morning light registered in Alex's brain, she was aware of the tickle. It was a sensation like a feather brushing lightly over her skin, starting at her toes and working its way upward. *A bug! There's a bug in my bag!* Alex thought frantically. *I will not freak out! I'll just slide out of the sleeping bag slowly and quietly.*

Alex was about to stick her head out of the sleeping bag when she realized that there was someone leaning over her. Someone who was humming softly to himself. And the tickle was moving in rhythm to the humming.

Alex peeped out over the edge of her nylon cover and saw Special Agent Lupo slowly passing a wand over her body. The wand had a heavy cable running from it to some kind of portable electronic device that Lupo carried in his other hand. The feathery sensation Alex felt was coming from the wand.

Lupo noticed that Alex was awake. "Good morning, Miss Mack," he said cheerfully. "Hold still for a minute more and I'll be done." The wand finished its slow sweep over her and Lupo switched it off. The tickle ceased immediately.

"Uh," said Alex. "Can I ask what you're doing?"

Lupo clipped the wand back to the side of the portable unit. "Just taking a baseline life-form scan. So when we look at our data later we can tell what belongs here"—he pointed to the ground and then pointed to the sky—"and what belongs *out there.*"

George Mack, setting the table for breakfast, caught the nervous expression on Alex's face. "Don't worry, honey," he said reassuringly. "It's a harmless procedure. I gave him permission. We've all been scanned already. If the agents didn't have to get such an early start today, I'd have had them wait until you got up."

"But I think they wanted to get out while it was still light," joked Ray from his place at the table.

"Very funny," was all Alex could think of to say to Ray. Inside her head, her thoughts raced. *I've got to talk to Annie. If I could feel that machine scanning me, what could it have found out about me?* Hoping to find her sister, Alex ran into the Runnamucka.

Annie was there, sitting at the little table. Agent Cabeza was there as well, and the two were chattering away about the "biological implications of broadcast power" or somesuch high-tech doublespeak. As Alex screeched to a halt in the doorway, they both looked up at her.

Agent Cabeza broke into a smile. "Good morning, Alex," she said. "I've been having a wonderful conversation with your sister. You must feel very lucky to have such a talented mind to talk to whenever you want."

"Uhh, yeah," stumbled Alex. "All the time. Especially now." Alex smiled tightly. "Annie, can we talk? Outside?"

Annie looked from Alex to Cabeza and back again, obviously reluctant to end her conversation with the FBI agent. "Sure. I guess so," she finally said.

As Annie got out from behind the little table, Agent Lupo's voice suddenly said, "Don't take long, though." Alex jumped. He'd walked right up behind her without making a sound! "I promised your father that we'd make up for our intrusion by taking you along with us when we go to town to interview the eyewitness."

Alex couldn't find anything to say, so she grabbed Annie's hand and pulled her sister out of the Runnamucka and on down toward the stream.

When they got there, Alex tried to whisper and yell at the same time. "Annie! We *can't* go *anywhere* with them!"

"Why not?" replied Annie calmly. "You've got something better to do? Agent Cabeza is a doctor as well as an agent. I'm having a great time talking to—"

"Annie, you don't understand! Agent Lupo scanned me while I was sleeping. And I *felt* it! He's gonna find out about me!"

Annie's eyes bugged. "You *felt* the scan?" Alex nodded. "Then we've *got* to go with them."

"*What?*" Alex screeched. "You *want* the government to take me away?"

"No, of course not! Listen to me. I don't know what data Lupo picked up on his scanner. Maybe nothing. So we've *got* to stay as close to them as possible. That way we can find out what they know and try to throw them off your track if they get too close."

Alex was silent for a long time, wrestling with her fears. Finally she said, "I guess you're right, even though it seems like walking into the lions' den. Or going out hunting with them, in this case. At least I'll have you and Ray to count on if something goes wrong."

Annie suddenly laughed. "Sorry, Alex, Ray's not going to be available today."

Annie's change in mood took Alex by surprise. "What's funny about that?" she asked, puzzled. "Is he going on another treasure hunt or something?"

"Definitely 'or something.' " Annie giggled. "He's going kite flying . . ."

"Kite flying," repeated Alex in a flat tone.

Then she felt annoyance rising. *"That's* more important than saving me from life in a secret lab?"

". . . with *Dad,"* finished Annie. She dissolved into laughter again.

A tart comment about Ray died on Alex's lips. Then, as the image of Raymond Alvarado and George Mack running around in the desert flying kites sunk in, Alex's dark mood shredded, blown away by the silliness of that picture. Soon she and her sister were laughing wildly as they walked back up to the camp. This was definitely shaping up to be the weirdest vacation Alex had ever been on.

The Federal agents' van was cramped with electronic gear and bizarre gadgets. Alex and Annie sat in the backseat wedged between an eighteen-inch parabolic microphone and a cardboard file box filled with reports of alien sightings.

The van had no air-conditioning, so the windows were rolled down during the trip into Dryrot. The combined noise from the engine and the wind roaring past made conversation a succession of shouts between the front seat and the back.

Alex eyed all the equipment with distrust. "Do you actually use all this stuff?" she shouted. "I thought the FBI was in charge of capturing kidnapers and serial killers and things like that."

Agent Cabeza turned to answer. "Actually, the FBI has the power to investigate any crime that breaks a Federal law, crosses state lines or threatens national security from within the borders of the United States. We can also help out in foreign cases where an American citizen is involved or where another country asks for our assistance. But like I told your friend Raymond, most of our work is just what we're doing today—running around interviewing people and filling out forms. In fact, that's mostly what I did before I transferred to this department."

"The government really takes flying saucer reports seriously?" said Annie skeptically.

Lupo answered this time, thankfully not taking his attention away from driving. "Let's say *I* take the reports seriously. The way I see it, somebody's got to look into all those things that are classified as 'unexplained phenomena.' Most of it turns out to be just that—cases that haven't been explained yet. Sometimes they're cases of other crimes that have been covered up, sometimes they remain mysteries." His eyes caught Alex's in the rearview mirror. "And sometimes we find cases that point toward things outside our normal experience. The truth is out there, somewhere."

"You said you drove in from that weird place called Area Fifty-one," yelled Alex. "Have you ever, like, found any real cases of illegal experimentation on people? Secret projects and stuff?" Alex ignored Annie's sudden glare.

Lupo shouted back over his shoulder. "If you want us to drop in on that chemical plant back home and shut them down, just give the word. We've done it before."

"Oh, stop pulling her leg, Lupo," Agent Cabeza told her partner. "People get nervous enough having a chemical plant near their town without making them think that every one is a hotbed of human experimentation or toxic waste production." She turned back to the girls. "Besides, we can't just drop in anywhere we want. There has to be suspicion of a crime or a complaint or report by a citizen for us to get involved."

"Which is why we're heading into Dryrot today," Lupo said as the town came into view on the horizon. "We spent yesterday scouting the area in general and arranging to have people gather in town today so we could interview the eyewitness and take scans of the locals who might be in the area we'll be checking out tonight."

A few minutes later, Lupo pulled the van up in front of the cafe. The last time Alex had been here, there had been only a few dusty pickup trucks parked in no particular order out front. Now there were at least a dozen dusty vehicles parked with even less organization than before. Lupo circled the parking area before giving up and parking on the bare dirt across the highway.

As she got out of the van, Alex looked at the empty highway stretching from horizon to horizon and at the single weathered building in view. Try as she might, she couldn't imagine living in a place so isolated.

She started to walk across the highway. "Don't forget to look both ways," Lupo cautioned.

Alex nearly tripped in midstep. *Out here?* she thought. *In the middle of nowhere? This guy's really spooky!* Then she smiled to herself. *But fun spooky.* Her mood suddenly lightened. *Let Annie spend the day talking to another superbrain, I'll stick with Lupo.*

Dryrot's cafe was just one section of the town's only building. A counter and a scattering of tables with chairs defined the cafe part, while the rest of the room was filled with the shelves of the general store and the desk for the mayor to sit at when the room played town hall. A small booth with a glass window filled one corner of the room—the town's post office.

There were about twenty people there when the girls and the Federal agents entered. All conversation halted and every head turned to stare at them. Alex felt an instinctual urge to duck behind something to avoid all those piercing eyes.

Nothing seemed to faze the two agents, though. Twin IDs flashed as they introduced themselves. Lupo said, "We appreciate the general turnout to welcome us, but to simplify our work, we'd like to speak with the eyewitness and the people living in the target area as a separate group."

There was some hemming and hawing in the crowd for a moment and then the mayor, a round man in the local flannel-shirt-and-jeans outfit stepped up to the agents and cleared his throat. "Since you were here yesterday, we had another eyewitness come forward."

"That's great," said Lupo. "We can use all the input we can find."

The mayor leaned in close to speak to Lupo confidentially. "There's input and there's input, if you get my drift. *This* input comes from our postmistress, Merry Munro. She's a fine lady and a good member of Dryrot. Works hard for the town. But—she's got some fixed ideas about some things."

"Things that have to do with our investigation?"

"Well," said the mayor, glancing up at the dark wood of the ceiling, "I guess that's for you to judge. All I ask is for you to give her a respectful hearing. We wouldn't like to see her get hurt by coming forward."

Lupo smiled reassuringly. "We're just here to

collect information, not to pass judgment.'' The mayor seemed to be satisfied with this, because Alex saw him shrug and then give a wave to the townspeople.

After a pause and a lot of shuffling around as bodies moved first one way and then another, there were only six people left standing in front of the agents. All the rest had shifted back to form a ring around the edges of the room.

Brandishing their portable scanning wands, Lupo and Cabeza quickly entered the six people who lived in the sighting area into their baseline database and then ignored everyone but the eye-witnesses. The spectators slowly settled them-selves back into the available chairs, leaving one table empty in the center of the cafe.

Alex and Annie sat side-by-side on a wooden packing crate and watched the agents sit down at the center table and set out a mini tape re-corder. Then a plump woman in jeans and a faded cotton work shirt sat down at the table opposite the agents. Her eyes were clear and her manner spoke of someone whom the desert had taught not to mince words. ''Meredee Munro,'' she said. "Most people here know me as 'Merry.' "

The agents repeated her name into the tape recorder and introduced themselves to her in turn. Lupo took the lead. "Ms. Munro. You say that you saw something in the desert yesterday?"

Merry set her face, stiffening her jaw. "I didn't need to see it." She tapped a finger on the side of her head. "I felt it. And I know why it happened, too." She pointed the same finger at Alex and Annie. "It was those kids. They're the reason behind all this!"

CHAPTER 7

Alex's heart stopped in her chest. *Is this it?* she thought. *Am I going to spend the rest of my life in a lab as a guinea pig?* She watched the agents carefully to see what they would do.

Surprisingly enough, the agents didn't even turn to look at the teenagers behind them. Lupo tilted forward over the table, staring intently at the postmistress. "Keep going," he said.

"The Space Brothers want them," Merry declared. "They've been coming to Fantasmas Mesa since before the Indians came. They take human children away with them to prepare them to be ambassadors when the time comes for Earth to take its place in the Galactic Brotherhood.'' Alex felt Annie relax and let out a sigh of relief as the older woman continued, ''We don't have any kids living out here anymore, so when these ones arrived, the Space Brothers came out of hiding to check them out.''

''If aliens made an appearance two days ago to attract the attention of some tourist kids,'' Agent Cabeza asked calmly, ''how did you come to know about it?''

Alex heard a rustle run through the crowd of spectators. She glanced over at them to see that a number of people were looking uncomfortable. When she looked back at the postmistress, Alex was surprised to see tears brimming in the older woman's eyes.

''They came for me once, when I was little,'' Merry said in a voice filled with heartbreak. ''They called me, in my head, in their sweet, gentle voices. I was too scared to go so they passed me over. But I've dreamt of them every night since then, and I can feel when they're near.'' She dabbed at her eyes with a red checked handkerchief and straightened up in her chair. ''I'm ready for them now, though. If they're back, I want to go with them. They have to take me. They *have* to."

Nobody in the room spoke for a moment. Alex noticed that all of the residents seemed to find the ceiling and distant corners of the room more important to stare at than their neighbor and postmistress. Finally Cabeza broke the silence. "Thank you for your time, Ms. Munro," she said politely. "We'll add your report to our files."

Lupo added, "I'm sure you would have made a wonderful ambassador, ma'am. Thanks for coming forward."

Merry searched his face for the slightest hint of sarcasm or scorn. Lupo's face remained sincere, however, so she nodded briefly and rose from the table. As she walked to the door of the cafe, the crowd parted before her, clearing a path. She paid no attention to this, her eyes looking out the door into the desert, seeing a lost destiny that no one else could perceive.

The second interviewee was a craggy-faced old man with a couple of days' growth of white beard beneath flashing, intelligent eyes. He wore dusty overalls and ancient, worn hiking boots. Even indoors he insisted on keeping his battered Stetson hat jammed down on his head.

Slowly and deliberately, the old man looked the Federal agents over, then extended his hand for them to shake. "George Hayes. Most folks call me 'Ravvid,' though," he drawled. "Pleased t' meetcha."

The entire room seemed to relax after Lupo and Cabeza shook Ravvid's hand. Alex watched with awe as the two agents slid smoothly into a tag-team routine, trading off questions to get the man's whole story.

Agent Cabeza started by asking Ravvid to repeat his identification for the tape recorder. The old man eyed her as if she hadn't been paying attention. "Like I said," he graveled, "George Hayes. Seventy-eight come next October. Got a little shack t'other side of Fantasmas Mesa. Spend most of m' time out lookin' fer the Lost Frenchman Gold Mine. Rest of it I sit an' think or play chess here with Mayor Carter."

"Loses most of the time, too," added the mayor.

"Let's see if I lose our bet on there bein' thunderstorms in the mountains tonight," Ravvid shot back. "I c'n smell 'em comin', sure enough."

"Yeah, and his dog predicts earthquakes, too," hooted the mayor.

"About the sighting," Lupo prompted.

" 'M gettin' to it," sniffed Ravvid. "I was checking out the west face of the mesa fer traces of the mine. Compasses act funny around there 'cause of some kinda metal deposits. 'S how it got its name—*fantasmas* means 'ghosts' or 'haunted' in Spanish. Indians thought it was some kinda playground fer spirits. Can't depend on survey maps, so the only way t' find anything out there is t' go over every square foot y'self. Started years ago on the east face an' been workin' my way around it counterclockwise since. May even get 'round the whole thing if I live long enough.

"Anyway, I've never seen any sign of haunts there, but two days ago I saw lights and somethin' flyin' through the air—all in broad daylight."

Alex held her breath. The canyon Annie had chosen for their experiments opened on the southwest corner of Fantasmas Mesa, and it sounded like, in contrast to the postmistress who had only imagined things happening there, old Ravvid had actually been just around the corner to the northwest of them.

"About what time did you have your first contact, Mr. Hayes?" prodded Agent Cabeza.

"Didn't say I had any *contacts*, Missy," Ravvid cautioned. "Don't think I'd have wanted to, in any event. Just saw and heard some mighty peculiar things in the sky."

Alex and Annie both let out a sigh of relief.

"The time?" reminded Lupo.

"Oh, early afternoon, I'd say. Sun was past overhead but not due t' set fer hours yet. I was rounding a pier—what you might call a promontory—when I heard a kinda clacking noise in the sky. Danged if there weren't a buncha rocks playin' billiards in midair a half-mile south of me!"

Alex sucked in her breath, remembering how she had described her play with the floating rocks with exactly the same term.

"Billiards? In the sky?" asked Cabeza.

"Well, not all orderly and racked out like on a pool table," corrected Ravvid. "But about eight t' ten good-size rocks floatin' a couple hundred feet up. There were these yellow flashes of light that seemed t' knock the floatin' rocks into each other. Like somebody or somethin' was playin' a game. Then there was a loud hummin' sound, like a generator on overdrive. Loud enough t' almost drown out a high-pitched screechin'."

Alex blushed, glad that Ray wasn't there to hear his reaction to the wasps described so embarrassingly.

"A few minutes later this flyin' saucer-shaped thing with golden lights exploding around the edges went sailin' up into the sky, till I couldn't see it no more. I headed on south, but it's pretty broken territory around there an' it took me an hour or so on foot. Didn't find nothin', though, so I hiked back home an' drove here t' tell Carter what happened. Guess whoever he told passed the word on t' you folks. It's a pretty bizarre story, I know, but it happened just like I told you, and that's that."

Agent Cabeza glanced at Lupo, then back to the old man. "Mr. Hayes," she began gently, "I realize you consider the desert your home, but there is a considerable body of evidence relating to mirages and heat-associated hallucinations—"

"Missy," Ravvid interrupted, fixing the petite agent with a withering stare. "I don't want to criticize you personally, but out here, a man's word is his credit, stock and soul." He cleared his throat and for a moment became a straighter, more formal figure. "I have a double Ph.D. in philosophy and psychology from Harvard. I spent thirty years teaching at the University of California at Berkeley before retiring to come live out here. I think I know the difference between what I witnessed and a mirage."

Cabeza blinked in surprise and sat back from the table a little. Alex thought she looked like she'd found a wasp when expecting a bee. Lupo broke in smoothly. "So, do you think you're ever going to find the Lost Frenchman Mine?" Alex recognized from Lupo's little smile that he was amused at his partner's confusion and was trying to hide it.

The old man shifted his eagle-gaze over to Lupo. "Of course not, son. It wouldn't be the *Lost* Frenchman Mine then, would it?" He softened. "Teaching was fun, but I got tired of it eventually. I couldn't imagine doing it for the rest of my life. Then one day I discovered the journal of a man who came looking for the mine sometime in the late 1800s. He never found it either, but I was deeply impressed with the way the desert changed how he thought and lived over the years. So I retired and moved out here myself. I'm happier now."

Some of the steam went out of him then, and he stood up slowly, as if his joints ached. He extended his hand again. "Thanks fer listenin' to me, an' I hope it helps you in your search. But I've got t' leave you with a question, son." He looked straight into Lupo's eyes. "Are y' sure you'll be any happier if *you* find *your* mine?"

He shook their hands and tottered out into the brilliant desert sunshine.

Alex saw Lupo stare after Hayes, his eyes thoughtful. Then he noticed Alex. He smiled his little half smile at her and winked broadly.

CHAPTER 8

The drive out of Dryrot was quieter than the one in. Lupo drove without speaking. Cabeza made notes in her case file and consulted a survey map of the area. Crammed again into the backseat, Alex and Annie relaxed a little. The old man hadn't seen them or said anything that actually revealed their desert experiments. It seemed that the job before them would be simply to make sure that the agents didn't find any evidence that would lead back to Alex.

Alex was more puzzled than her sister about the postmistress, though. *By their reactions, the townspeople already knew about Merry's fixation on the "Space Brothers,"* Alex thought, *but they treated her as one of themselves anyway. Does that mean that there's a chance I could live a normal life, even if my secret got out?* Of course, Meredee Munro only imagined things. She wasn't almost an alien herself. And she didn't have Danielle Atron sniffing at her trail.

Cabeza navigated Lupo from dirt road to dirt road, taking the van well south of the Mack camp and curving northwest toward Fantasmas Mesa. The van jounced and rattled over an old wooden bridge spanning the ravine that cut through the desert between the mesa and the camp. As they neared the mesa, Annie tugged at Alex's sleeve and pointed out the window. High in the air near the horizon bobbed two tiny, brightly colored kites. They dipped and spun in the midday sky and both girls grinned, thinking of their father and Ray at the ground-end of those invisible strings.

Finally Cabeza announced that they had come as close to Ravvid's viewpoint as roads would let them. Lupo stopped the van and everyone clambered out for a much-needed stretch. The agents opened the back doors to the vehicle and started pulling out bundles of long, light poles. The poles were topped with gadgets that reminded Alex of little graduation caps set on top of four suction cups, each facing a different direction.

"These are solar-powered omnidirectional bio-sensors," said Cabeza to the girls as she divided the bundles up into four equal batches. "I'm going to start from the approximate location Mr. Hayes first noticed the incident. Agent Lupo is going to start from a point on the far south side of the presumed incident site. Since we're splitting up, you girls have to decide which of us you're going to pair up with."

Alex had a definite preference but she hesitated to speak first. Luckily, Annie immediately walked over to Cabeza and hefted a bundle of the sensor poles. Cabeza seemed pleased, and Lupo looked at Alex. "Well, I got the partner I wanted," he said, winking at her. Alex felt herself blushing.

Annie and Cabeza each shouldered a bundle of sensor poles and struck out into the brush toward the mesa. Lupo took both remaining bundles and tossed them into the backseat. He held the passenger door open for Alex and gestured at the seat. "Your coach awaits, mademoiselle," he said with a smile.

Alex hopped in and barely had her door closed before Lupo was in the driver's seat and revving the van up. Without looking at his copy of the map, he navigated unerringly back the way they had come, turned left at a fork in the road, and brought them to an area that was suddenly familiar to Alex. It was a shallow ravine that cut across the path toward the box canyon. The site Annie had picked for their experiments was a mere quarter-mile away.

Once again, Lupo was out of the van and hauling out the sensor pole bundles before Alex had the door completely open. "This is where we start walking," he said to her. "Grab these and let's hike."

Alex shouldered her poles and scurried to keep up with Lupo, who was already several yards ahead of her. She had just caught up with him when he stopped unexpectedly and took a bearing on the van behind them. "We might as well start here."

He took a pole from his bundle and in one swift motion sank its pointed bottom a foot into the desert soil. He sighted along the pole back to the van and then turned to face the opposite direction. He pointed ahead with one finger. "We'll start a circle heading south first, then work our way back north along the mesa," he said, his finger describing an arc. "Then we'll head back toward the van and hopefully finish up just as Cabeza and Annie complete their circuit from the north."

Lupo checked to make sure that the pole was set firmly and then moved quickly forward into the brush. Alex realized that his habit of jumping ahead as soon as something was done could work in her favor. She shot as small a zapper as she could produce at the little biosensors atop the pole. Then she scurried quickly to catch up with Lupo before he set the next pole.

Once they settled into a rhythm, the next hour passed quickly. Lupo would find an appropriate site to plant a sensor and then move on, and Alex would zap it lightly before she left. The first few zaps were a tug on her conscience, but she soon decided it was a necessary tactic. *Lupo and Cabeza are nice as people*, she thought. *But it's my life and my family's that will suffer if anybody finds out about my powers. They're nice enemies, but they're enemies all the same. We can trust no one with my secret.*

To Alex's relief, Lupo didn't lead her anywhere near the little box canyon but concentrated his attention on the mesa, focusing his sensors on the massive upthrust of stone. When the agent's bundle of sensors was exhausted, he announced that they'd gone as far as they needed to and now it was time to circle back.

"Can we stop for some water first?" asked Alex. "I'm thirsty."

Lupo looked shocked for a moment, as if the thought of human frailty came as a surprise. Then he was all concern and comfort, unclipping a canteen from his belt and handing it to Alex. "Sorry," he said, grinning. "I keep forgetting about the real world when I get going."

"I understand that," agreed Alex. "Everybody thinks I live in another world most of the time, too. Their favorite phrase is, 'Earth to Alex!' "

"Well, it'll get better," said Lupo cheerfully.

"Either you'll grow out of it, or you'll find a way of making a living at it, like I did."

"Can I ask you a personal question?" ventured Alex hesitantly.

Lupo shrugged. "Government regulations usually discourage us from having personal lives and thoughts, but I'll give it a shot."

Alex suppressed a grin. She had a serious question. "Agent Cabeza and Annie seem to have hit it off really well," she told Lupo. "They're both such superbrains. Do you ever feel, like, overwhelmed working with someone so bright?"

"Actually, people seem to have a harder time dealing with me than Cabeza, but I know what you mean." Lupo took a swig of water from the canteen and stared out into the desert.

Encouraged, Alex went on. "You say you went to school with my dad, so you know that he's a genius. I think Annie was born quoting formulas. Even my mom is a real go-getter, do-everything kind of person. Sometimes I feel so hopelessly . . . ordinary."

"Ordinary's not bad, Alex," Lupo said, still staring out onto the endless desert vista. "In fact, when you've seen as many strange things as I have, ordinary is like a breath of fresh summer air." He grew thoughtful. "In a way, what Cabeza and I do is try to make the world safer for ordinary people, so that they can live peaceful, uncomplicated lives."

"But ordinary's so *dull!*" complained Alex.

"Well, that may be a sign that you're not ordinary after all. Most people have something special inside them that others can't see. Sometimes it takes a long time for that specialness to grow, but if it does—if it grows strong enough to survive and mature—you become a truly nonordinary person." Lupo turned to look Alex in the eye. "Listen to me straight. Without good grounding in a nice, ordinary life, there's a real danger that too much specialness can turn a person into a monster. I've met some monsters out there. Treasure your ordinariness as long as you can."

Lupo stood up suddenly and recapped the canteen. "You've almost got me telling you campfire boogie-stories in broad daylight. It's time for us to get back to work if we're going to make our rendezvous."

* * *

The hike back seemed to take less time than the trip out, in spite of the fact that neither Alex nor Lupo had any further conversation. Even at that, Cabeza and Annie were at the van before Lupo and Alex arrived.

The two agents unpacked a collapsible antenna, stuck it on the roof of the van and then began wiring it into a heavy transceiver in the back. Alex dragged a fascinated Annie over to the far side of the road.

"I zapped all of our sensors as we went," whispered Alex. "Did you do yours?"

Annie dug a heavy metal block out of her pocket. "When Agent Cabeza wasn't looking, I ran a magnet over the solar panels and the bio-sensors. I don't know exactly what it'll do, but I'm sure that skewed readings will confuse things."

A shout from Lupo interrupted their conference. "We're ready to run our first tests, if you girls want to see it." Alex and Annie trotted back to the van.

Agent Cabeza was crouched in the cargo section of the van, hooking a cable between the transceiver and a computer array bolted to the van's inner wall. "The biosensors are preset to detect and record the life-signs of anything larger than a coyote," Cabeza explained. "We've already fed all of the scanning data that we recorded into the computer. That will allow us to subtract any normal readings from what the sensors pick up. Whatever's left will be either a larger animal, like a bobcat or deer—easy enough to identify—or . . . something else."

"Let's do our first run and see how things look," said Lupo, flicking switches on the transceiver. Alex and Annie held their breaths as the machine began to hum.

Lupo looked puzzled at the readouts. He beckoned Cabeza over and her brow furrowed as well. "That's all wrong," Cabeza said and twiddled a few dials. Alex's heart leaped to her throat. *Have we been caught? Can they tell we tampered with their sensors?*

Lupo explained over his shoulder as he and his partner continued to adjust the machine. "The sensors aren't responding properly," he said. "They should at least have activated as we planted them and then sensed us as we moved, but all we recorded is static."

"There seems to have been some kind of electromagnetic interference with every sensor we put out," concluded Cabeza. "Try sending a reset code."

Lupo toggled a switch as the girls watched nervously. "Partial success, Cabeza," he reported. "We've lost about a third of the sensors, mostly in my sector. The others are back on line, but they show nothing outside of the baseline data, which includes us. Someone or something interfered with our probes as soon as we set them out."

"That can mean only one thing," said Cabeza. Alex's heart stopped cold, and Annie grabbed her hand and squeezed nervously. Luckily neither of the agents looked at the Mack girls. Instead, they stared out at Fantasmas Mesa.

"Somebody—or something—doesn't want us to know they're here," finished Lupo.

"Pay dirt!" whispered both agents in unison. An echo of distant thunder seemed to underscore their words.

CHAPTER 9

Alex walked along the stream by the Mack camp, moodily kicking small rocks into the water. She and the others had arrived back home to find Ray and her father still out flying kites. Her mother had immediately wanted to know what had gone on in Dryrot, and Alex had left it to her sister and the agents to fill her mom in on the morning's activites.

Alex wanted no part in retelling what had occurred because she hadn't yet sorted out how she felt. A walk along the stream and then into the brush around the camp felt like a good thing to do. She pondered her situation as she went.

At home, the business of having special powers and hiding them seemed like a game, she thought. *But out here, being alone with the possibility of having the government chase me . . . that's different. It's* scary!

I always thought that having powers was a kind of magical nuisance—sort of like pimples. It's embarrassing and weird, but I always figured I'd come to terms with it sooner or later. But this is me! *I'm going to be like this for the rest of my life, unless Annie figures out some way to make me normal again. I'm always going to be different.*

Now, different's not always bad—I wouldn't really want to be the same as anybody else. And some kinds of different can be good. Annie has a brain like nobody else, except maybe Dad. Ray is different, too—he wants so much to be able to do everything, he has a hard time limiting himself to just one thing.

Alex scaled the far side of the ravine and began walking aimlessly through the brush. Somewhere in the back of her head was an important realization, if only she could reason her way to it.

I wouldn't mind being good different. I guess I'm just scared of being bad different—of having people laugh at me or be scared of me.

That woman from Dryrot today, now she's bad different. Not many people go around saying that they're waiting for aliens to take them to a better place. She's lucky to be out here with people who care about her. If she showed up back in Paradise Valley, she'd be a laughingstock. But what makes her difference not as good as Annie's or Ray's?

That question had no easy answer for Alex, so she kept walking and thinking. She crested a small rise and was shocked out of her pondering by the sight of a human figure sitting on a rock a couple hundred feet away. Alex recognized the person as Merry Munro, the postmistress from Dryrot.

Merry sat with her back to Alex, her face turned to the distant rise of Fantasmas Mesa, purple now in the westering light. Alex remembered the woman's statements to the agents and realized that she was waiting outside the Mack camp because she believed that the "Space Brothers" would show up again, looking for teenage ambassadors.

Alex's heart went out to her. *She seems so sad. She's spent her life waiting for something that will never happen. I wish there was something I could do for her.*

Her eyes widened. *Maybe there is*, she thought.

Alex held her breath and concentrated. She felt her body shift form, leaving behind the rigidity of bones and flesh for the supple flexing of liquid. In a moment, she had morphed to her liquid state and was slipping over the hardpan of the desert toward Merry Munro.

She circled around through the brush until she was between the seated woman and the mesa she faced. Then she flattened herself as thin as possible and slithered up to the rock. Alex willed her liquid form to stand up into a transparent version of a human form, but not one that was recognizable as Alex Mack or any other person.

The postmistress's eyes snapped open and her jaw dropped in shock and disbelief. Alex spoke to her in a gurgling, inhuman voice. "Meredee Munro."

Merry leaped to her feet in alarm. "Wh-who are you?" she stammered.

"I am the one you have been waiting for," said liquid-Alex.

Tears of joy spilled from Merry's eyes. "You

came for me? After all these years? You're finally going to take me away with you?"

"Your place is not with us. Your place is with your fellow humans."

Merry shrank back. "But why? I wanted to be your ambassador to my people. Is it because I'm too old? Why did you make me wait?"

Trying to put a warm tone into her gurgling voice, Alex held out a watery hand-shape. "You are our ambassador already, Meredee Munro. You have told your people about us for years. But our time has not yet come. Your people are not ready for us. It is your job to help prepare them."

Alex could almost feel Merry's emotions churn like stormy water. A creature of her dreams had finally appeared—but only to tell her she could not join them. But it had also said that there was work for her to do on their behalf. Alex watched as Merry fought back her tears and squared her shoulders. "What do you want me to do?"

Alex had thought hard about this while slithering up to the Dryrot postmistress. "I want you to help your people to care for your planet, to make it ready for our arrival. Encourage your people to work for peace, to clean up your world, to banish hate and fear. If we took you with us, you would be one small voice among the stars. Here, you will teach your people to sing a song of hope and promise, and become a mighty chorus, singing in harmony to greet us when our time finally comes."

Merry digested this for some moments. Then she smiled. "I'll do it," she said. "People think I'm crazy because I believe in you. They can't think I'm much crazier if I tell them to live in peace and cherish their planet." In a soft voice, she added, "Thank you for coming to me."

"We could do no less," said Alex. Then she flattened herself too quickly to be seen and slithered rapidly away.

Merry blinked in surprise and looked around for her transparent visitor. When it became clear that she was alone, the postmistress sighed deeply and slid off her perch. She turned her back on the mesa and walked away, back toward her car and her life in Dryrot.

Alex watched her leave from the shelter of a creosote bush. When the woman was gone, she morphed back to her human form. *The important thing about being different*, she thought, reaching the conclusion she had been groping for before, *is what you do with your difference.*

A sense of satisfaction rose in her and buoyed her up all the way back to camp.

When Alex arrived, she found that Ray and her dad had returned and that the elder Macks had gone off for a drive before dinner. Annie was just finishing updating Ray on the morning's events. The three teenagers were sprawled along the campside streambed, talking quietly in the shade provided by the small scrub oaks.

"After all that, the agents still think there are aliens here?" sputtered Ray.

"Convinced of it." A grim-faced Annie nodded. "They're taking naps now so they can go out prowling tonight. You should have seen them in action, Ray, Agent Cabeza especially. I really believe that they won't leave as long as there's the slightest chance of finding what they're looking for."

Alex's adventure with Merry Munro had driven the dilemma of the agents from her mind until now. The threat came rushing back to her.

The agents were actually *encouraged* by the mystery of their malfunctioning equipment. It might be only a matter of time before they discovered *her* part in that sabotage. And when they finally got to compare all the scans they had collected—how could they not discover her secret?

Annie looked over at her sister as if noticing her there for the first time. "Where have you been off to?" she demanded.

Alex gave her sister and her friend a quick rundown of the show she'd put on for Merry Munro. Annie was scandalized. "You actually turned to liquid and talked to her?" she said. "You must be crazy!"

"I had to do something!" Alex said. "I couldn't just let her wait there forever." She thrust out her lower lip. "I only gave her what she wanted."

Annie had no room for sympathy. "That's the stupidest thing I ever—"

"Wait, that's it!" interrupted Ray. "We'll give the agents what they want!"

"What?" Alex was still smarting under the whip of her sister's anger. Had she missed something?

"Look," Ray said, standing up and starting to pace along the stream. "They came here because somebody thought they saw aliens, right?"

"Yeah, so?" asked Alex.

"Well, that means if the *aliens* go away, *they'll* go away, *too*—or at least follow where they think the aliens are going."

"But, Ray," cut in Alex impatiently, "there *are* no aliens—just me!"

"They want to find *aliens*." Ray grinned as he squatted down in front of the two girls. "So let's say a flying saucer takes off from here tonight and just happens to fly away . . ."

"The agents will go chasing after it!" Annie sat up, inspired.

"Real simple, Ray," said Alex. "If there were some aliens to fly away. But there aren't, so it's a dumb idea."

"No," said Annie, standing up and dusting herself off. "It's a brilliant idea! If you can be an alien for Merry Munro, you can be an alien for Lupo and Cabeza." Alex looked at her sister in confusion. "Come on, let's see what kind of stuff we've got to build a flying saucer!"

*   *   *

The last hours of daylight were spent quietly assembling an odd assortment of gear and transporting it in batches to the box canyon site. Ray's overstuffed duffel provided a roll of Mylar he had packed to build and repair kites with, and a Park Service emergency kit contributed a bundle of emergency flares. As the kids worked, the skies over the mountains to the north darkened and faint thunder rolled across the desert with increasing frequency.

As they finished their preparations, Alex listened to the thunder and said, "Looks like old Ravvid's going to win his bet with the mayor."

"Come again?" said Ray, confused.

"Never mind," said Alex. "Let's get dinner ready. Mom and Dad'll be back soon." There was nothing left for them to do but to wait for darkness to fall.

CHAPTER 10

Agents Lupo and Cabeza declined the Macks' offer of dinner when they woke up, saying that they'd already packed sandwiches for their night's vigil. As the sun set, their van disappeared over a hill trailing a cloud of dust.

George and Barbara Mack were tired out from their day's touring and were only too happy to let the kids clean up the remains of dinner. "In fact," said George Mack, "I think your mom and I are going to sack out early tonight. What are you planning for the evening?"

"Ray brought along a telescope," said Annie

brightly. "I was hoping you'd let us borrow your binoculars so we could do some stargazing."

"Of course you can," replied her father. He addressed his other daughter. "You know, Alex, I can't say how pleased I am that you and your sister are doing so many educational things together."

To avoid life in a test tube, thought Alex, *I'd stick to Annie like glue, Dad.*

Thunder rumbled in the distance. Barbara Mack looked worried for a moment. "Don't go too far, now, and pay attention to the weather."

"No problem there," chirped Ray, holding up a black, phonelike device. "All-band CB walkie-talkie *with* built-in weather channels." He looked over at the full moon rising on the clear eastern horizon. "Anyway, it's only raining in the mountains, not down here."

"Still," said George Mack, "it's better to take precautions and avoid trouble."

We took precautions and trouble came looking for us anyway, thought Alex as her parents kissed her good night.

The adults went to bed and the kids pottered around the camp, cleaning up after dinner and rebuilding the fire to last well into the night. George Mack's gentle snoring echoing inside the Runnamucka was the signal that the coast was clear to start their secret mission.

The moon was high and bright enough that Alex had little difficulty following Ray and Annie's lead as they wove their bikes through the chaparral toward the box canyon. Alex thought that the desert at night was a truly spooky place. Her heart skipped a beat every time a jackrabbit or other small animal broke from cover and raced away from the intruders. Off to the north, the sky occasionally lit up with bright flashes as the storm battered the mountains miles away. When the thunder arrived, many minutes later, it sounded like the grumbling of a restless giant. A wind was rising, rushing northward as if anxious to join the activity up in the mountains.

Their path wound around the southernmost sensor pole that Alex and Lupo had set up earlier that day. Alex eyed it with suspicion as they rode by. "Hey, Annie," she called ahead to her sister. "What are we supposed to do about these biodetector thingies? Won't they tell the agents that we've been here?"

"Not according to what Agent Cabeza told me," Annie answered. "Our bioscans are already in their computer. It's supposed to ignore anybody who's already on file. It's only programmed to flag anything that's *different.*"

Annie may have felt reassured by that, but Alex still feared that her GC-161-altered body would be *different* enough to catch the computer's attention.

The crunch of tires braking on gravel pulled Alex back into focus. In the clear moonlight she could see the rocky walls of the little box canyon. *It all started here,* she thought. *I guess it's as good a place as any to try to end it.* She came to a stop and shrugged off her backpack.

Annie was carefully setting out supplies in the clearing while Ray, true to form, simply upended his pack, dumping his load on the ground. Alex wished she could do the same, but the annoyed look Annie shot Ray made her empty her pack as neatly as her sister.

Without any idea of when the agents might patrol this end of their target area, Alex and Ray, under Annie's direction, worked as fast as possible. Their first need was for local materials. A quick trip to the nearby ravine brought them to a stand of young bushes. Annie selected long, springy saplings and branches for Ray to chop down with his camping knife and Alex to gather into bundles.

The gurgling noise of the stream in the ravine seemed louder to Alex than she remembered. She called softly to her sister, "Annie? Is it just me, or is the water level higher than it was before?"

Annie paused a moment to study the stream in the moonlight. "It's definitely higher," she said, finally. "The runoff from the mountains must be heading this way already." She did a quick survey of the bundles and announced, "It looks like we have enough. Let's get out of here before it gets too dangerous to be down here."

Back at the mouth of the box canyon, Alex used Ray's knife to cut away forks and twigs from the branches to make thin, flexible poles. Then she peeled the bark off some of the poles to make a pile of long strips.

Ray took the poles and laid them out in a rough circle on the ground. Annie followed behind him and used the bark strips like twine, tying pole ends together firmly. "The key to succeeding with our trick is to use as much natural material as possible," she said. "That way, there won't be any evidence left behind that can be distinguished from the ordinary stuff that grows here."

Soon, there was a circle of tightly bound poles roughly twenty feet in diameter lying on the ground. Annie kept muttering calculations under her breath as she and Ray worked to lay straight poles from one edge of the circle to another, cross bracing the circle and creating a strong, lightweight disk.

When the disk was done, all three teenagers used Ray's roll of Mylar to stretch a surface onto the wooden frame. Ray smeared fast-drying glue along the rim of the frame and along the edges of the Mylar where they overlapped. Ray surveyed their creation as he brushed dirt over his hands to cover the sticky spots. "It's not the best kite I've ever built," he said, "but it is the biggest and weirdest-looking one."

"We're not done yet," said Annie. "We still have to rig a support for the payload. Get the nylon twine."

The kids carefully stood the enormous kite on edge and flipped it over so that the Mylar surface was facedown. The lifting surface was too fragile to step on, so it was Alex's job to use her powers to float pieces of twine over to where Annie wanted them and then concentrate hard to tie the twine tightly to the center of the frame.

Ray, meanwhile, was tying flares to the rim of the kite, being careful to create a symmetrical arrangement. Following Annie's design, he made sure that the flares were fastened to the kite rim along their lengths, rather than at right angles. He was also sure to have all the flares arranged head-to-toe. He wasn't sure exactly what this was for, but Annie was very insistent on this pattern, and too much was at stake to question her at this late date. Annie had also instructed him to cut the flares down to mere three-inch stubs. "We don't want to set the desert on fire," was her only explanation.

Finally the great kite was finished and it was time to attach the payload—the thing that Annie was counting on to make the jerry-rigged structure fool the Federal agents into thinking that this was a real UFO. Ray stripped the base of his uncle's metal detector off its handle and handed it to Annie. "I hope you can make sure we don't lose this," he said, nervously. "My uncle would kill me if I didn't bring it back."

"That'll be Alex's job," Annie replied as she tied the battery-operated sensor to the improvised basket that hung from the kite's center. "She's the one who has to float it back down."

"But how can I float it back?" said Alex. "I couldn't keep the rocks in the air when I wasn't looking the other day."

Annie took her sister by the shoulders. "You *have* to, Alex! It's the only way we're going to pull this off." She put the metal detector into Alex's hands. "Hold it. Feel it. *Memorize* it! Make it a part of your mind so that you can feel it wherever it is. You don't actually have to float it. You just have to *call it back!*"

Alex stared at the metal disk in her hands, opening her mind to explore it. She tried to feel and identify what made this piece of metal unique and different from anything else. She put it down on the ground and then walked across the clearing. She closed her eyes and spun in a slow circle. Without opening her eyes, she tried to locate the metal detector.

There it is!

She felt filled with new hope. "Got it!" she shouted.

"Great," said Annie, "because now you've got to help Ray climb the cliff."

"I knew I was gonna hate *some* part of this," groused Ray as he sorted through his pile for his strap-on shoe spikes.

Alex giggled. "This is the guy who was going to be the great explorer?" she teased. Before Ray could answer, she continued. "Don't worry. I'll backstop you as you climb. If you slip, I'll hold you in place by floating you until you get a grip again."

"Sure you couldn't just float me to the top?" Ray asked hopefully as he tied the spikes onto his hiking boots. Then he answered his own question. "I know—you gotta save your strength. Been nice knowing you."

The three teenagers walked over to the rocky wall of the box canyon. Annie handed Ray the walkie-talkie, which he clipped onto his belt. She took the other one and made sure that they were working and tuned to the same frequency. "Remember," she told him as he slung the binoculars around his neck. "Your job is to find a nice, safe ledge to sit on where you can scan for the agents' headlights. As soon as you see them head this way, give us a squawk to let us know." Annie hugged him. "Good luck and be careful."

"Aye, aye, Cap'n." Ray saluted with a grin. He turned and started climbing up the hill.

Alex and Annie held their breath as they watched Ray climb. It seemed to take him an eternity to move upward. The canyon wall rose at a comfortable climbing angle and the full moonlight clearly showed him every hand- and foot-hold. Alex kept a light mental touch on Ray, ready in an instant to push him up or to throw a force shield under him if he slipped. But her powers were not needed, and soon Ray was halfway up the mesa and firmly seated on a wide ledge.

The walkie-talkie squawked. *"Eagle-Eye to Ground Control. Sir Raymond has conquered Everest! Out."* Ray's joke broke the tension and both girls laughed.

Alex took the other walkie-talkie and pushed

the "speak" button. "Eagle-Eye, this is Golden Girl. Good job. Brain Wave and I will proceed with Phase Two. Out."

Annie gave Alex a sarcastic look. "Golden Girl? Brain Wave? Are you sure that Mom and Dad didn't just find you on the doorstep one day?"

Alex sauntered back to the kite. "How do you know *you* weren't the Z-Mart blue light special?"

Alex's joke covered her real nervousness. The rest of the night's work was hers and would take all the concentration she could muster. She closed her eyes to make sure she could still feel the location of the metal detector. *Yup*, she thought, *still there*.

Alex and Annie carefully lifted the great kite and balanced it on edge. Annie also held the fishing reel-like spool of kite-flying line that they would use to control the kite once it was airborne. "Remember now," Annie instructed Alex, "you lift the kite until the wind catches it and then I'll guide it up to the right height. When I give the signal, start your stuff but save your strength for the grand finale when the agents show up."

Nearly two years of practice with her levitation powers lent Alex confidence as she tensed her mind and lifted the enormous kite up into the air. Within seconds, it was a hundred feet above her and Annie was yelling, "I've got it! I've got it!"

As Annie played the line out, pulling with all her might against the powerful lift of the kite's flying surface, the walkie-talkie slung from her belt squawked.

"I see headlights moving slowly about a mile due west!"

Without taking her attention off the kite, Annie yelled to Alex, "Go for it!"

CHAPTER 11

Alex concentrated and created the largest swarm of zappers that she had ever made. She sent the golden sparklers rushing up to meet the kite and stuck them to the rim and to the support rods. From the ground, it looked like a swarm of giant fireflies had just taken flight and then decided to self-destruct in a blaze of glory high over the desert floor.

Once she was sure that she had drawn enough attention to the skies for anyone watching them to notice, Alex fired another zapper at the metal detector as it hung swaying beneath the kite. She sent it into the control switch assembly and then followed with more in a rapid sequence. There was no way Alex could feel it, but Annie had assured her that the zappers would not only turn the detector's magnetic coils on and off, but make the magnetic waves it generated shift in power in a random way that was sure to catch the attention of the agents' detectors.

It was a good thing that Alex couldn't spare any attention to look over at Annie. Her sister was fighting a losing battle to control the kite. Annie, of all of them, had known how powerful the lift of all that stretched Mylar could be and several tugs had already lifted her completely off the ground. It was only a matter of minutes before either the line broke or Annie was hauled up into the sky by the kite.

Ray's voice crackled through the night. *"Headlights just made a sharp turn. They're following the old dirt road toward you. Over."*

That was Alex's cue to move onto the next part of the plan. She lit the cut ends of the flares with zappers. Immediately, the flare stubs ignited and began spewing red fire. Since all the burning ends were facing the same direction, their thrust soon set the kite spinning.

Now came the hardest part. Annie cut the kite line with the knife, leaving Alex to hold it in place and continue to flicker the metal detector on and off. With the kite solely under her control, Alex could suddenly feel the strength of the winds whipping through the sky above. Again and again she had to strain against gusts that wanted to flip the kite over or send it spinning out of control to disappear in the north, where lightning was ripping the sky more and more often.

Alex could hear Annie chanting time—"twenty one-thousand, twenty-one one-thousand, twenty-two one-thousand"—and she wondered if her strength would hold out long enough to make sure that Lupo and Cabeza got a good fix on the "UFO."

Alex's body was trembling with the effort when Annie finally slapped her on the shoulder and shouted, *"Now!"* Alex immediately reached out with her mind for the memorized feel of the metal detector. She had no time to spare to guide the machine back. She just yanked it to her as hard as she could.

The kite filled all her attention now. She helped the flares spin the kite even faster and sent the whirling disk soaring up into the sky with all her might. In seconds the fiery streamers had receded to a dot high in the heavens.

One by one, the distant flares burned out their short lives. Annie had planned that the short stubs would only burn for a few minutes. That was the signal for the last act of their play. With a mental wrench, Alex tore the Mylar to shreds and burst the bark strips holding the frame together. In a moment, there was nothing left of the "UFO" except invisible debris to be swept into oblivion across the wide desert.

Alex collapsed to the ground, unaware of the tears streaming down her face. She turned to look for her sister and found Annie scrabbling at a hole in the ground next to Alex that hadn't been there before. Annie tugged hard and pulled up her prize—the metal detector—a little worse for wear, but back safely from its journey.

Annie looked at the short distance between the metal detector's impact crater and where Alex had stood. Fear was written all over her face. "Uhh . . ." she said. "You didn't have to cut it *that* close!" Only then did Alex realize that when she'd yanked the metal detector back to herself she'd been in danger of the thing actually *hitting* her when it landed.

Relief swept over Alex like a roar and she hugged Annie. They'd done it! Now they could only hope that the agents would buy the "UFO's" departure and chase it elsewhere, leaving the Mack family in peace.

Another roll of thunder boomed out of the north and nearly drowned out Ray's voice from the walkie-talkie. *"Hey!"* he said. *"I just lost the headlights of the van. They disappeared down by the bridge that crosses the ravine!"*

Just then the automatic emergency frequency of the walkie-talkie cut through Ray's voice.

"Mayday! Mayday! This is Special Agent Lupo! Our vehicle has fallen into a ravine! We are injured and need assistance! Anyone within range please help! We are at—" The rest was lost in static as lightning ripped across the sky in a blinding flash. Without warning, rain began to fall.

CHAPTER 12

No further messages came from the walkie-
talkie.

"We've got to help them!" Alex shouted to
Annie. "No one else knows where they are! They
could die out there!"

Alex could see Annie struggle with the choice.
To show up so suddenly could destroy their
careful plan to distract the agents away from
Alex. But to not help could be worse. Much
worse.

The sound of rocks and gravel tumbling down
the canyon wall made both girls whirl in unison.

Ray came sliding down the last of the scree seat-first, heedless of the danger in climbing down without a backstop. He ran straight for his bike. "Let's move!" he shouted.

That was the spark the girls needed. Leaving the kite-building materials where they lay, they jumped on their bikes and followed Ray into the chaparral, the light rain beading their faces.

To Alex's surprise, once they reached the closest of the sensor poles, she found that she could clearly remember the path she and Lupo had taken when planting them. She pedaled into the lead and guided Ray and Annie, counting off the poles as she passed them.

It was a race against time, because scudding clouds kept smearing past the full moon, obscuring its guiding light and making riding treacherous. But soon they found the old dirt road and Alex unerringly led them to the right, searching for the old wooden bridge that spanned the ravine. Even at this distance, though, they could hear the ominous gurgling of water on the move.

The moon was behind a cloud when they found the bridge. They saw no trace of the agents or their van, only a muddy torrent that had overflowed the banks of the tiny stream and broadened to soak the entire bottom of the ravine. *Did I make a mistake?* wondered Alex. *Did Ray see them disappear on a different road?*

Then the moon cleared and a groan of metal rose from the ravine north of the bridge. In the clear light, Alex could now see the skid marks where the van had missed the curve onto the bridge and slid through the brush into the ravine.

At the same moment, Ray pointed toward Fantasmas Mesa. A spot of bright light kept winking on and off on the cliff wall. It kept repeating the same pattern—three short, three long, three short. "Look," shouted Ray. "It's Morse code. They're sending an SOS!"

As gusts of wind blew sheets of light rain through the air, the path of the flickering light beam appeared and disappeared. It was soon clear to the three teenagers where the beam's source was—nearly a hundred yards north of the bridge.

They walked their bikes quickly through the path the van had carved through the chaparral and soon came to the edge of the ravine. The van had spun around as the driver had tried to brake and had fallen tail-first down the steep incline. The back doors had sprung open, spilling equipment and gear into the mud of the streambed, and the back wheels poked out from under the chassis at odd angles. "They broke their rear axle," said Ray.

Agent Cabeza sat precariously on top of the front windshield, aiming a powerful halogen flashlight at the mesa, doggedly sending out the SOS. Agent Lupo had a loop of electrical cable tied around his waist and was trying to scramble up the side of the ravine, his legs soaked in water and mud. He was using only his right arm—his left hung at a painfully awkward angle at his side. Several gouges in the mud and slumped piles of dirt showed where he had unsuccessfully tried to climb out of the ravine.

"Agent Cabeza! Agent Lupo!" shouted Alex. "Are you all right?"

"Alex? Alex Mack?" Lupo shouted back, unable to see the kids yet. "Is that you?"

"Yes!" Alex shouted. "Annie and Ray are with me. We heard your call and followed your light. Are you hurt?"

"Don't come near the edge!" Lupo warned. "It's too unstable! Agent Cabeza slipped on it and gave herself a concussion. I dislocated my shoulder in the crash. Go back to your camp and get your dad to drive out here."

There was a low vibration building in the ground under their feet. Annie's eyes widened in alarm at the sudden rise of the water at the bottom of the ravine. "There's no time for that!" she shouted. "There's probably a flash flood headed down the ravine already from the storm! You'd drown before we made it back! We've got to get you out *now!*"

In spite of the danger of the moment, Alex noticed that Agent Cabeza hadn't reacted at all. She kept flashing her SOS at the mesa like a robot programmed for only one task. *If she hit her head and got a concussion, it's a miracle she can still sit up. It must be taking all her strength to keep sending that signal.* There was no question of leaving either of them down there.

Ray took the lead now. "Throw us your line and we'll pull you out! It's your only chance!"

Lupo looked back at Cabeza and then up at the teenagers. "I guess you win. Here goes!" He unlooped the cable from his waist and threw it toward them with all his strength. It fell short. "It's no use. I can't make it!"

Annie hissed urgently to Alex. "Never mind our secret. *Help* him!" Alex gritted her teeth and nodded. To Lupo, Annie yelled, "Try again!"

Lupo gathered the cable for another try and threw again. This cast was weaker than before. But Alex reached out with her mind and snagged the cable in midair, pulling it up to where Ray and Annie could grab it. "We've got it!" yelled Ray.

Lupo was too tired to recognize the impossibility of his success. "Tie it around something," he called. "I'll rig a harness for Cabeza!"

Annie and Ray pulled as much of the cable up as they could, wrapping it around the trunk of a nearby scrub oak and knotting it as best they could. Alex tested the cable and then announced, "I'm going down there to help them."

"No!" shouted Annie.

"You're crazy!" added Ray.

"Look," insisted Alex. "I'm the only one who can do it. I'm the lightest of us and I'm the only one who doesn't need muscles to get them out of there. You guys have to be up here to haul on the line."

Alex could see that Annie positively hated the idea and Ray was not happy with it either. But the rumble under their feet reminded them that they had precious little time to argue.

Alex didn't wait for their agreement. Keeping a hand on the cable so Lupo wouldn't notice, she scrambled down the crumbling wall of the ravine to land by the wrecked van.

Lupo was gently taking the flashlight out of Agent Cabeza's hands when Alex joined him. This close, Alex could see the bruise that darkened the fair skin of Cabeza's forehead and the trickle of blood that disappeared into her black hair. She let Lupo slide her off the van and into Alex's waiting arms. Lupo seemed to see Alex for the first time. "Hunh," he grunted. "Are things special enough for you now?"

Alex didn't answer. Instead, she concentrated on helping Lupo rig the end of the cable into a rough harness around Cabeza's waist, wincing in sympathy every time Lupo banged his dislocated shoulder.

When the harness was as secure as it could

be, Lupo told Alex, "You go up with her, I've got to salvage our equipment." Before Alex could argue, Lupo disappeared into the van.

Well, thought Alex, *it's probably better that you don't see this, anyway.*

"Pull her up, Ray!" Alex shouted up the ravine. When the cable tensed up and started tugging Cabeza up the wall, Alex created a force shield under the limp agent and pushed it as hard as she could. She hoped Ray would feel the change in tension and reel her in quickly.

Her hopes were answered when Ray and Annie both hauled on the line and pulled the near-weightless agent to safety. A moment later, the loose end of the cable dropped back down into the ravine.

"Lupo!" she yelled. "Cabeza's safe. We've got to leave *now!*"

Lupo crawled out of the cargo section of the van, his good arm clutching a box of disks and tapes. "Take these! I have another batch to get and then I'll go!"

A roar like a freight train approaching drowned out Alex's reply. She snapped her head around to the north in time to see a wall of water twenty feet high crash into the curve of the ravine not a hundred yards away from the van. The impact barely slowed the onrushing flood. Instead, the water chewed an enormous section of the ravine wall into mud and added it to its already swollen and churning bulk.

There was no time for argument—there was barely time to act. Alex grabbed Lupo by the part of him that was nearest, which unfortunately for Lupo was his dislocated arm. Alex felt a sickening "pop" as the shoulder moved back into its socket and the pain made Lupo pass out. His body went limp and Alex had to grab onto the door frame with her free hand to keep his deadweight from dragging her down into the van.

The wall of water hit the van just as Alex lifted Lupo and herself up and away from the doomed vehicle. Muddy spray drenched them both and knocked the box of tapes out of Lupo's hand. Even the spray had the impact of a brick wall, and Alex found herself and her burden being swept along the ravine.

The world swept dizzyingly around Alex, fogging her concentration. Then she remembered—she was heading at high speed directly for the old wooden bridge! If she didn't pull herself and Lupo up to the bank, they were doomed.

This had easily been the most strenuous night of Alex's life. She had used her powers more often and stretched them further than ever before. She felt that she barely had an ounce of strength left. *But if I don't find the strength, somewhere,* she thought, *we're* both *goners!*

She concentrated mightily to morph both herself and Lupo at the same time. She felt her shape dissolve and flow into her watery form. A tugging all along one side told her that the unconscious Lupo was now as liquid as she. All she could see was the brick footings of the bridge zooming toward her. Then there was only a jumble of spray, crashing metal and . . . limp oblivion.

CHAPTER 13

Bright sunlight pierced Alex's closed eyes, making her wince. *I'm getting to hate morning in the desert*, she thought sleepily. *Who wants to wake up just because the sun is rising?*

Something seemed odd about that thought to Alex, but she couldn't quite place what. She heard her mother whisper in a strained tone, "It looks like she's waking up." Other hushed voices muttered around her.

I'm not waking up, groused Alex to herself. *I'm trying to sleep. I've been having this dream about saving Lupo and Cabeza from a flash flood and I want to go back to see how it turns out.*

Sudden realization almost as sharp as the morning sun flooded Alex's brain. She and her friends *had* saved Agent Lupo and Agent Cabeza from a flash flood! Or had they? Alex didn't remember anything after the torrent of water hit the van.

Alex could feel that she was lying in her sleeping bag on some hard surface. She could also feel that every inch of her body seemed to have its own collection of bruises. Now that she was more awake, she could feel that it even hurt to breathe.

A cool shadow fell over her, blocking the light. Alex tried opening her eyes and succeeded, after a moment of wincing. She blinked tears away and the shapes of her mother and father came into focus as they leaned close. "Mom? Dad?" Her voice sounded like a croak to her ears.

"Alex, we're so glad you're all right!" George Mack said, his eyes brimming with emotion.

Barbara Mack lifted her daughter's hand and kissed it. "Everything's okay now," she said. Then her brow furrowed. "How could you give us such a scare like that? What were you doing out in that ravine after we warned you about how dangerous it was?"

Alex knew things must be better than they seemed if her mom could relax enough to yell at her. She closed her eyes again.

"Hey," broke in a smooth male voice. "That's no way to wake up a heroine." Lips pressed briefly against her forehead and Alex opened her eyes to see Special Agent Lupo bending over her. The lanky agent's left arm was secured in a sling and what was exposed of his arms and face was dotted with small bandages. "After all," Lupo smiled at her and continued, "if it weren't for the three of them, Agent Cabeza and I wouldn't have survived last night."

Alex's heart skipped a beat. *How* am *I going to explain how we rescued them without revealing my powers?*

Ray's voice broke in. "Hey, it was just luck that we were out stargazing when we heard your Mayday and saw your signal light shining on the mesa. Once we found you and got a line rigged up, getting you out of there was a cinch."

Alex looked up into Lupo's face. They both knew that there had been more danger involved than that. Lupo winked at her and she knew that they had entered into an unspoken conspiracy— what George and Barbara Mack didn't know couldn't frighten them.

Alex struggled to sit up and found no shortage of hands to help her. She'd been laid out in her sleeping bag on top of the picnic table. Beyond the awning, the fierce light of the desert sun cast small shadows directly below objects. Alex had slept until nearly noon! Ray's mention of the signal light jogged her memory. "Where's Agent Cabeza? Is she okay?"

"She's gonna be all right," a different voice answered. Boot heels clumped on the concrete pad as a short figure in jeans, battered hat and a plaid work shirt walked over to Alex. "Mayor Carter?" said Alex, recognizing Dryrot's elected leader.

"Doctor Carter, at the moment," he said, whipping out a small penlight and checking Alex's pupils with it. "Officially, I'm a veterinarian, but I do people-patching on the side. Folks ain't much different from animals, when you come down to it." He flashed a grin. " 'Course, animals complain a dang sight less."

Carter took Alex's pulse and prodded her ribs gently with a meaty finger. "Looks like you're gonna be all right, too," he said. "The lady agent had a slight concussion that'll need to be followed up at a hospital when she gets back to a city, but for now, she's doing fine."

Carter stood back up and tucked the penlight away in his shirt pocket. He addressed Lupo, who was by the water tap, using a wet rag in a vain attempt to remove mud that stained his pants up to the knee. "What do you want me to do about your van?" Carter waved one hand lazily toward the road.

Alex followed his gesture and saw a flatbed towing truck parked behind the Runnamucka. On the bed, secured by a tow-chain and nylon tie-downs was what remained of the agents' dark van.

The vehicle was dripping mud and looked as if a giant had first squashed it and then bent it into a hairpin shape. The glass was gone from all the windows and one of the rear doors was gone, ripped off at the hinges. From what Alex could see, no equipment that hadn't been bolted to the chassis remained, and those pieces left appeared broken and caked with thick ooze.

Agent Lupo stared at the van without speaking for a moment. Then he shrugged. "It's a total loss, like all our data," he said sadly. "But I know that the Bureau will want to see it for themselves. Just tow it back to town and we'll have a government truck pick it up after we check back in with our office."

It was only then that Alex noticed the hand-lettered sign on the tow truck's door. It read, C. CARTER'S TOWING AND HAULING, DRYROT, CA. She looked at Carter. "You're the cafe owner, the doctor, the mayor *and* you own a tow truck?" she asked in wonder.

"The only one in town," replied Carter. "That's why they keep electing me mayor. That way, nobody else has to work." He stared hard at Alex, a sly twinkle in his eye. "I like Dryrot to be a quiet town. You try and keep the excitement down for the rest of your stay, hear?" He tugged the brim of his hat by way of farewell to the crowd and was soon backing the flatbed away from the camp.

Lupo stood without moving as his ruined van

disappeared into the distance. Alex walked over to join him. "I'm sorry you lost all your equipment," she said quietly.

Lupo looked down at the mud stains on his pants. "I don't remember you kids pulling me out of the flood last night," he began. "But I know that Ray rode his bike back to camp and your dad drove out to bring us all back. I had him drive me back at first light so I could see what I could salvage. There was nothing, nothing but yards of mud and splintered boulders. All our tapes, our computers, our files—all gone."

He turned to face Alex then, a strange light in his eyes. "But we saw it, Alex!" he continued. "We saw it take off and fly away. Maybe it went home. Maybe it just moved to another place. But Cabeza and I will go back and wait for another sighting. And then we'll follow that one, and the next and the next. Someday, we'll time it right and we'll meet them and then we'll have our proof."

Alex was awed by the intensity in Lupo's voice and the way his absolute conviction so clearly painted a picture of how he would spend his life. "How can you do it?" she asked. "You almost died and you lost everything. How can you just pick up and do it again?"

Lupo sighed deeply before answering. "Sometimes, Alex, you get to choose what you are, what you want to do with your life. Sometimes life decides for you what you're going to do— and all you can do is try to do the best you can." He looked down at her. "Maybe that's the difference between being ordinary and being different. We don't get to choose." He looked back at the desert horizon.

When Lupo didn't say any more, Alex quietly walked back to the Runnamucka.

As she stepped into the shade of the awning, Annie and Agent Cabeza climbed down out of the motor home. The petite agent's head was swathed in an elastic bandage, with a thick gauze pad covering a good portion of her forehead. On seeing Alex, Cabeza reached out to shake her hand. "I want to thank you for what you did for us last night." She fished a crumpled card out of her pocket and pressed it into Alex's hand. "If you ever need anything, anytime— don't hesitate to call."

Cabeza turned to Annie. "Your parents are going to drive us into Dryrot to wait for other agents to come pick us up. If you decide to change your mind, give me a call." She walked out to join Lupo. "We're ready to go, Mr. Mack."

George and Barbara Mack appeared by the 4WD, holding the doors open for the agents to climb in. George shaded his eyes to look at his daughters, and called out, "We'll be back in an hour or so. *Please* try not to get into any trouble while we're gone!" Without waiting for an answer, he got in the car and drove away.

Alex's strength suddenly gave out and she swayed on her feet. Annie caught her and carefully led her down to the shade by the streambed where Ray was already lounging in a fold-up chair. "Looks like we pulled it off," was his greeting to Alex and Annie.

The girls settled down by the gurgling water and for a moment, nobody spoke. Then the peace of the area revived Alex enough to remind her of Agent Cabeza's odd comment to Annie. She turned to her sister and asked, "What was Cabeza asking you to change your mind about?"

Annie made a wry face. "She wanted to know

if I was interested in applying for a job with the Bureau. I told her no."

That cracked Ray's cool. "You *what?*"

Annie grinned a little. "I told her that life as an agent seemed a little too adventurous for me. I said that beakers and chemicals and formulas were all the excitement I wanted out of life."

Everybody laughed and Ray settled back in his chair. "I can't believe you passed up a career like that." Nobody spoke for a moment. Then Ray announced, "Well, I know what I want to do for the rest of the vacation!"

The girls groaned.

"Nothing!" Ray shouted. "Lots and lots of quiet nothing."

"Amen," said Alex, and let the burbling of the stream lull her to sleep.

About the Authors

DAVID CODY WEISS and BOBBI JG WEISS are writing partners. They're also married. And they have lots of cats. Day after day they slog away at their computers, wracking their brains to write up fanciful and often absurd stories that they then sell to publishers for money. They have written a whole lot of stuff, among them novels (*Are You Afraid of the Dark?: The Tale of the Shimmering Shell; Star Trek: The Next Generation: Starfleet Academy: Breakaway* and *Star Trek: Voyager: Starfleet Academy: Lifeline*), novel adaptations (*Sabrina the Teenage Witch* and *Jingle All the Way*), comic books (*Pinky and the Brain, Animaniacs*), trading cards (*Batman and Robin, Star Trek Universe, James Bond Connoisseur Collection*), and other weird stuff like clothing tag blurbs, office catalog copy, and little squeezy books for kids who can't read yet so they just look at the pictures and squeeze the squeezy toy.

Bobbi and David hope to be filthy rich one day because laughing all the way to the bank sounds like fun.

Sometimes, it takes a kid to solve a good crime....

Original stories based on the hit Nickelodeon show!

#1 A Slash in the Night
by Alan Goodman

#2 Takeout Stakeout
By Diana G. Gallagher

#3 Hot Rock
by John Peel
(Coming in mid-August 1997)

#4 Rock 'n' Roll Robbery
by Lydia C. Marano and David Cody Weiss
(Coming in mid-October 1997)

To find out more about *The Mystery Files of Shelby Woo* or any other Nickelodeon show, visit Nickelodeon Online on America Online (Keyword: NICK) or send e-mail (NickMailDD@aol.com).

A MINSTREL® BOOK

Published by Pocket Books

1338-01

A MINSTREL BOOK

Simon & Schuster Mail Order Dept. BWB
200 Old Tappan Rd., Old Tappan, N.J. 07675

Please send me the books I have checked above. I am enclosing $_____(please add $0.75 to cover the
postage and handling for each order. Please add appropriate sales tax). Send check or money order--no cash
or C.O.D.'s please. Allow up to six weeks for delivery. For purchase over $10.00 you may use VISA: card
number, expiration date and customer signature must be included.

Name _____

Address _____

City _____ State/Zip _____

VISA Card # _____ Exp.Date _____

Signature _____ 1053-13

"Welcome to Good Burger, Home of the Good Burger, Can I take your order?"

GOOD BURGER™

When a new burger joint opens up across the street from Good Burger, the competition is on!

Can Ed save Good Burger from Mondo Burger?

A novelization of the movie from Paramount and Nickelodeon

Based on the popular skit from Nickelodeon's hit TV show *All That*

<u>In Stores Now!</u>
Get your copy while it's hot!

 A MINSTREL® BOOK

Published by Pocket Books

 Paramount Pictures presents in association with Nickelodeon Movies
Good Burger
Coming to theatres soon!
© 1997 Viacom International Inc. All Rights Reserved

To find out more about *All That* or any other Nickelodeon show, visit Nickelodeon Online on America Online (keyword: NICK).

1383